ROMANCE IN THE AIR

After ending a relationship she discovered was based on lies, Annie Layton has sworn off men. When her employers, Edmunds' Airways, tell her they're expanding, she eagerly agrees to help set up the sister company. Moving up north will get her away from her ex — and the Air Ministry official who's been playing havoc with her emotions. But Annie hadn't known exactly who she'd be working with . . . Will she find herself pitched headlong into further heartache?

•

•

• F
t
U
• Th
Ins
• Tw
Opl
• The
Aust

You can
by m
Every co
would l
require

THE U
The C
Le

website: w

46 810 292

PAT POSNER

ROMANCE IN THE AIR

Complete and Unabridged

LINFORD
Leicester

First published in Great Britain in 2014

First Linford Edition
published 2015

A catalogue record for this book is available
from the British Library.

ISBN 978–1–4448–2553–4

Published by
F. A. Thorpe (Publishing)
Anstey, Leicestershire

Set by Words & Graphics Ltd.
Anstey, Leicestershire
Printed and bound in Great Britain by
T. J. International Ltd., Padstow, Cornwall

This book is printed on acid-free paper

1

Oh drat, thought Annie, as she became aware that a car had pulled up alongside her. She'd been so absorbed in her self-imposed task she hadn't heard it approaching.

'Can I do anything to help? Are you ill?'

It was a deep-brown voice — warm and toe-curling. Annie's heart raced as she straightened up.

'No, thank you, I'm all right, I was just . . . ' Her words dried up as her eyes met those of the owner of the voice and to her dismay she felt a warm blush staining her cheeks. Even sitting at the wheel of the car — a big, black, expensive-looking vehicle, of a make she couldn't put a name to — and even though his eyes didn't match the warmth of his voice, he exuded a chemistry which hung over him like an aura.

His hands, big and square, rested casually on the steering wheel. The sleeves of his logan green sweater had been pushed up slightly, revealing a sprinkling of fine, curly black hairs on his arms.

Annie sucked in a deep breath. It wasn't the fact he'd score high on the Hunk Richter Scale causing her loss of speech and her blush, was it?

Of course not. It was the thought of telling him *why* she'd been crouching in the middle of this lonely stretch of road in the pouring rain. She'd have reacted the same way if it were Mr Slightly-Below-Average sitting there.

She was small, he observed, not petite; her curves were well-rounded. He couldn't help but notice that. Her ribbed sweater clung to her like a second skin. A wet skin. He dragged his glance upwards. She was blushing. The delicate colour brought her face alive. He wanted another glimpse of her smoky grey eyes, but she'd lowered them and was looking down at her hands, one clasped almost protectively over the palm of the other.

'You were just . . . ?' he prompted.

'I was just moving a snail,' she mumbled. 'It's all right, you can continue your journey. I don't need any help. Thank you for asking, though,' she added.

Like a child remembering good manners, he thought. And however appealing she seemed, she *was* young, though she must be over seventeen if that parked car was hers.

'Rather a dangerous thing to do, stopping in the middle of the road in this weather.' He pointed over his shoulder with his thumb. 'I presume that *is* your car?'

Annie nodded, and then wished she hadn't as rivulets of raindrops trickled down her face. And *he*, darn him . . . she felt sure he was trying not to smile.

Embarrassment swirled through her in waves and she replied snappily, 'Actually, it's you who are stopped in the middle of the road. *My* car is only a foot or so from the verge. And — '

'Well, at least you had the sense to put your hazard lights on.'

Annie glared at him. At least, it would have been a glare if the raindrops on her eyelashes hadn't made her blink. 'As I was saying . . . if I hadn't stopped exactly when and where I did . . . I, or someone else, would have driven over it.'

She looked lovely when she was annoyed. And perhaps she wasn't as young as he'd first thought. If he didn't live at the other end of the country . . . *What was he thinking?* He had more important things to concentrate on. Dating was not on his list.

'I'm sure other drivers would appreciate your action should they know of it,' he said. 'Nasty things, nails.'

Before Annie could correct him, he did the almost-smile thing with his mouth again; then he glanced in his mirror and pulled smoothly away.

She watched the car disappearing into the distance until a cold stream of water running down her back brought her to her senses. Then, letting out a long, low breath, she squelched her way to the edge of the road.

She stepped gingerly into the ditch, which ran alongside the road then stretched up to place the snail safely under the hedge. 'Do you realise the embarrassment you caused me?' she said. 'And do you think he really thought I'd stopped to move a *nail?*'

Annie laughed as the snail poked his head out from under his shell. 'No, I don't know, either,' she said. 'Bit of an enigma, the man with cold eyes and a warm voice.'

His eyes weren't exactly cold, she mused, as she got back into her car. They were sort of soulless and empty, as though he'd had some recent tragedy in his life. But she'd had enough problems of her own without wondering about someone else's. Especially as he was someone she'd never see again.

She wriggled on the seat. 'Literally soaked to the skin,' she muttered. She'd have to go back home to get dried and changed and . . . she glanced in the mirror at the mass of dark red corkscrew curls dangling like pigs' tails, *wet* pigs' tails . . . and do something with her hair. It was a good job she hadn't fixed a definite time to see Gail.

★　★　★

Annie pulled into the car-park allocated to Edmunds' Airways. She sat for a moment and glanced at the other cars, mentally conjuring up pictures of their owners; the usual passengers had obviously taken their regular Wednesday flight to London.

That was the beauty of a small airline like this — people could be treated as people, every passenger became an individual. And tomorrow she'd be a part of it all again; returning to the job she loved. Oh, was she glad to be back.

For the first time in weeks — no, months — a feeling of near-contentment settled over her. True, the shadows were still there; they were fading, though, and now everything was about to get back to normal, they would fade even more.

That was all she wanted. To get, and keep, her life on an even keel. No problems, no unpleasant surprises — and definitely no emotional entanglements. Cupid and his pesky arrows could take a break. A permanent one. She'd have her work and her friends and that would be enough.

The rain had turned to a light drizzle, not heavy enough to warrant an umbrella. Annie got out of her car and locked it, then hurried across to the modem building that was the pulse of Edmunds' Airways.

Walking into the room which comprised arrival and departure lounge and check-in, plus security, immigration and customs areas, she breathed in the familiar aroma of coffee, plastic and people.

She smiled as Hildy, the pretty Dutch receptionist, greeted her enthusiastically.

'Welcome back, Annie. Are you sure your ankle's all right?' Without waiting for a reply, Hildy continued, 'It's been hectic here the last few days. Gail took on the Amsterdam flights, but she's got an important meeting tomorrow. I was having visions of *me* having to be flight attendant.'

Annie laughed. 'You'd have had to do everything walking on your knees,' she said. 'Imagine trying to get your five-feet-nine along the aisle of a Dornier. Even I have to bend down when I demonstrate the life-jacket procedure. Where's Gail now, Hildy? In the office?'

'No, she's showing somebody over our new joyrider. Some high-up big bod from the Air Ministry, I think, come to check things over. Let's hope he approves of what he sees; it would be awful if he found something wrong when we're all set to celebrate Edmunds' fifth birthday tonight.'

'Yes, let's hope he doesn't turn out to be a monster of menace,' Annie said.

'He's rather different from the usual

officials we get,' Hildy continued. 'This one's really dishy. He's tall with it, too. I didn't have to lower my head to talk to him.' She glanced through the large plate-glass window behind her. 'Look over there,' she commanded Annie. 'You'll soon see what I mean.'

Annie sauntered over to the window. The Air Ministry official had his back to her; but even from here, his broad shoulders, lengthy back, narrow hips and long legs looked impressive, and Annie could guess at the powerful muscles underneath the dark, well-fitting suit.

Her gaze wandered upwards. His thick black hair was streaked here and there with silver, she noted, gazing in a dreamy way at the gap between his hair and the collar of his suit as he bent his head towards Gail Edmunds. *Nice kissable back of the neck.*

Where had that thought come from? She'd obviously been reading too many romantic novels during her enforced time off. Earlier on she'd let a plangent voice and eyes that hinted of tragedy temporarily affect her power of speech, and *now* she had goosebumps because another male happened to have an appealing neck. After her last experience she was off men for good.

That experience still had the power to hurt and, although it had happened over three months ago, it was all too easy to recall how she'd felt. Shuddering, she pushed the unwelcome memories away. Yet she was still staring through the window.

It was all right saying she was off men for good, but she couldn't tear her eyes away from that tall figure; she was longing to see if his face matched up to the rest of him. He turned then, as if he'd felt her intense gaze, and with a sense of shock Annie recognised him.

Suddenly, her bones felt as though they'd turned to mush. Even at this distance he was exuding that air of chemistry she found hard to ignore.

'Rubbish,' she muttered firmly and, shrugging, she turned away to face

Hildy. 'As you said, he's rather different from the usual officials, much richer if his car's anything to go by. I wonder where it is? I didn't see it in the parking area.'

'How do you know anything about his car?' asked Hildy.

'I also know he's got a rather nice logan green sweater that he doesn't seem to be wearing now,' Annie said. 'He must have had his suit jacket on a hook in the car, ready to replace the sweater when he got here.'

'You've lost me,' said Hildy.

Annie took pity on her and went on to explain what had happened earlier when she'd met the official.

'At least he didn't hear me talking to the snail afterwards,' she added, once Hildy had stopped laughing.

'I can just see the headlines now.' Hildy started chuckling again. ' 'Air Ministry Official states that flight attendant is unsuitable for the job because she talks to nails'.'

'If it *had* been a nail and I'd known

an A.M. official was about to drive along that stretch of road, I'd have left it there for his precious car to go over.'

'Don't look now, but he's just come in with Gail,' said Hildy. 'Oh, they've stopped; I was hoping they'd come over.'

Annie couldn't resist turning her head.

Her eyes met his immediately. He seemed to be studying her with a curious intensity. But there was also something else, too. She felt as if an invisible thread was stretched out between them, a thread drawing them closer even though neither of them was moving.

This really was ridiculous; like a voiceover in a bad movie describing how it felt when the female lead met a stranger's eyes across a crowded room. She'd be hearing birds singing and bells ringing next.

She forced herself to look away and went across to the coffee machine. As she opened her bag and took out her purse to find the appropriate coins for the machine, she was aware of Hildy's look of surprise.

Everyone at Edmunds' knew Annie's views on the coffee from the machine. She liked strong Turkish coffee, not this weak apology for a drink.

Wrinkling her nose in disgust at the sight of the pale liquid in the plastic cup, she wandered over to the reception desk. 'I suddenly felt very thirsty,' she told Hildy.

Then, determinedly keeping her back to the rest of the room, she continued to chatter in a desultory way to the receptionist.

Annie knew even before Gail arrived at the reception desk that the Air Ministry official had left the building. Knew from the easing of tension in her body and by the way that funny feeling — the one a person gets at the back of their head when someone's looking at them — had disappeared.

'Annie, welcome back, love. I'm sorry you had to wait.'

Annie laughed and returned Gail's

hug affectionately. 'I didn't mind wait-ing. I enjoyed soaking in the old familiar atmosphere.'

'You didn't enjoy your drink, though.' Gail pointed to the still-full plastic cup on the reception desk. 'Throw it away, Annie. I left some really strong coffee percolating in the office.'

★ ★ ★

Annie took a long drink of coffee then smiled across the desk at Gail. 'So, how is everything? Tell me all the news. The last three months seemed like three years. I just can't believe how stupid I was . . . ' Annie rolled her eyes. 'I mean, fancy tripping over my own front doorstep and ending up with a broken ankle. I was stone cold sober, too.'

'It was lucky for all of us Katie had been covering your holiday leave and was willing to stay on after your accident,' said Gail. 'Even though she did leave us rather abruptly.'

The last sentence had sounded like a

question. Annie fiddled with her empty coffee mug. She didn't want to talk about her sister's sudden departure.

It was obvious Gail was curious, for she continued, 'I know you were due back next week anyway, but Katie seemed to have settled in so happily with us, didn't she?'

Annie nodded. 'She did, but she's always tended to do things on impulse.'

'I was going to ask her if she'd consider staying on permanently. It can be quite a headache finding someone who has the right attributes and also measures less than five-foot-two.'

'Why were you going to ask Katie to stay on? Is someone leaving?'

'No. It's just that . . . well, I can't say too much yet, but we're thinking of maybe taking on a partner and expanding.'

'Is that why you got the new joy-rider?' Annie asked. 'Will it be operative soon? I noticed you showing the visitor from the Air Ministry over it.'

'The Air Ministry . . . ? Oh . . . er . . . yes.'

Annie was surprised by Gail's flustered manner and to see a faint blush colour Gail's cheeks. 'So you were aware of the M.F. too? 'Magnetic Force',' she explained, noticing Gail's querying look. 'Such charisma. But it's probably all on the surface, you know. And I meant you were aware of it, too — as in, as well as Hildy,' she added quickly and rather confusedly, inwardly cursing the fact she'd betrayed any interest in the man.

'Of course you did,' Gail said, deadpan. 'He mentioned the two of you had met earlier. He was surprised when I told him you were one of our flight attendants. He thought you were about eighteen and much too young for such a responsible job.'

Annie laughed. 'It's no wonder he thought that really. One, I looked like an orphan in a storm; and two, when he discovered I was old enough to be a flight attendant, he probably couldn't imagine me being . . . ' Annie quoted one of Edmunds' mottoes: ' . . . 'Polite to passengers at all times'.

'Anyway, that's enough about him.' *More than enough.* Even talking about him was enough to make her forget she was off men for good. 'Which shift am I on tomorrow?'

They sat for a while longer, going over the rota, then Gail said briskly, 'Right, now that's sorted, I'm going to dash through the rest of my workload and then go home to make myself look something like decent for tonight.'

'You always look good and you know it,' retorted Annie, getting to her feet. And, after promising to see Gail at the party, she hurried out of the office.

'He's not here,' Hildy said, obviously noticing the way Annie's eyes flickered round the room. 'He came back in for a while, but now he's gone.'

'Who has?' Annie prevaricated.

'Mr Air Ministry official. I think I've changed my mind about him. Honestly, Annie, the way he was looking at you when you went to the coffee machine made shivers run down my spine. He might be tall, dark and dishy, but there's something almost dangerous about him.'

'Rubbish. He was probably just working out what to write in his report, or whatever it is officials do with the information they ferret out. Besides, dishy or dangerous, we won't be seeing him again. By now, he's most likely on his way to stir up some airline at the other end of the country.'

* * *

Driving home, Annie wondered about the expansion Gail had hinted at. Could they be adding extra routes? Getting another aircraft? Surely they'd need more space if they were adding extra routes? And it must be something like that, or Gail wouldn't have mentioned wanting to keep Katie on.

Unwillingly, Annie's thoughts turned to her sister. She'd managed to steer Gail away from the question of Katie's surprising departure. And clearly Gail wasn't aware that Katie hadn't been living at home since the end of August. Not since she'd moved into a flat provided by her latest conquest — one of Edmunds' regular passengers. Gail wouldn't have been so keen to keep Katie on if she'd known that.

Annie couldn't understand her sister's attitude. Katie had told her the man in her life was separated from his wife. Had said she didn't mind he wasn't really free. 'It's fun being the other woman, Annie. I get all the pluses and none of the minuses. You should appreciate that.'

Yes, Annie thought, Katie actually dared to compare what she was knowingly doing with what happened to me. But that was over and done with. History.

As for Katie, Annie hadn't spoken to her for weeks. Not until she'd phoned on Saturday to say everything in her life had changed. She was leaving the area, moving on.

'And I'm glad Katie has gone off somewhere,' muttered Annie, driving into the garage attached to the house.

'If she's unhappy she's brought it on herself.' But deep inside, Annie felt concerned about her sister, and wished she knew where she was now.

As she opened her front door, Annie noticed a snail gliding over the Virginia creeper that covered the walls of the house. She decided to leave it there. Look what had happened the last time she moved a snail!

But once indoors, her thoughts returned to the man who owned the big black car.

As she swished a few drops of neroli oil round in her bath water, she tried telling herself she was only thinking about him to prevent thoughts of the not-distant-enough past.

The trouble was, she hadn't had enough of anything else to occupy her mind lately. That would soon change, what with tonight's party and then getting back to work tomorrow. She'd be meeting other people again and there'd be no room in her mind for unhappy memories.

Or for thoughts of a tall, dark, official with eyes that burned into her. A man who'd thought she was too young for such a responsible position.

She climbed into the bath and lay back in the warm, scented water. It was just as well she wouldn't be seeing him again; she might have been tempted to show him how *irresponsible* she could be.

A vision of herself placing a snail on the roof of his car popped into her head and she smiled. Snails made a strange squeaking noise when they moved on a smooth, shiny surface. Wouldn't he be worried if his beautiful car developed a squeak he couldn't trace?

That wasn't a good thought, though, because she also had a vision of him moving round the outside of the car, running his fingers over various parts, and he had such nice hands. He had a nice body, too, and a voice that made her toes curl, and . . . *Heavens, Annie. That's enough.*

She was glad to hear the phone

ringing just then. Usually, if it rang when she was in the bath, she let the answer-phone take over. Not this time, though. Talking to whoever was phoning her would take her mind off *him*.

2

Although the private function room in the Old Manor House was crowded — as well as the airline staff and their partners, some of their regular passengers had been invited to celebrate Edmunds' fifth birthday — Zak spotted Annie the second he walked through the door.

He made his way across the room and came to a halt a short distance behind her and her friends. Then, leaning unobtrusively against a pillar near the end of the bar, he listened to the joking banter.

'Love the dress, Annie,' said Hildy. 'It's — '

'Tantalising,' growled the man next to Annie. 'She wore it especially for me. For my plan.'

'He got me out of my bath to tell me about it,' said Annie. 'I mean, his phone call did. And, because I was dripping wet, I agreed to let him take me to the Farmer's Arms before we came here.'

'I had to bribe her, though. I came up with something I knew would do the trick. I promised her an Illicit Affair.'

Zak felt his face tighten. Was that clown really talking about having an affair with Annie?

'Why did you want her to go to the Farmer's Arms with you, Garry?' asked Hildy. 'Mind, I'd have gone with you if it meant getting a helping of that divine dessert they do there.'

So they were talking about food. Zak let out the breath he hadn't realised he'd been holding.

Garry spoke again. 'I wanted to be seen with someone who looked tantalising to make my true love realise that she did love me after all.'

The other female in Annie's group joined in the ridiculous conversation.

'To make your true love realise Annie loved you?'

Not funny. Zak choked down a spurt

of anger. *Steady*, he warned himself. It's just party talk. It doesn't mean anything.

Annie was perturbed to discover she wasn't really enjoying the frivolity. She felt decidedly uncomfortable. But why? She was used to the way Garry clowned around. He was one of Edmunds' ground engineers; he was like an older brother to her, and they had a long-standing platonic friendship, going back five years to their first day of working for Gail and her husband, Martyn.

Had she lost the knack of socialising? Spent too much time alone the last three months? *Pull yourself together, Annie*.

'Poor Garry,' Annie said. 'He was really upset when the one who's giving him a hard time wasn't in the Farmer's Arms. Or maybe he was upset because he had to buy me a drink,' she added. Then she hugged his arm and joined in the laughter that followed her remark. Garry was renowned for his generosity.

Zak could only see Annie's back view. He tried to read her body language when he saw her squeeze the arm of the wisecracking guy. Just a friendly gesture, or what? And did it matter, anyway?

What was it about her, for heaven's sake? When he'd spoken to her on that stretch of road, her attitude and appearance had amused him. OK, he'd noticed her femininity, but he hadn't felt this . . . this *need* to know more.

Then an hour or so later their eyes had met through the huge plate glass window behind Edmunds' reception desk, and there'd been that flash of . . . of surprised recognition between them. Because, in spite of her transformation from a drowned rat, he'd recognised her immediately.

But his only thought then had been that she'd come to meet someone off the return flight from London. Until he and Gail went inside, and Gail had told him who she was . . .

Of course. What he felt now was

professional interest. It was nothing to do with knowing she was a good few years older than she looked. He needed to find out for himself if Annie Layton lived up to Gail's commendation.

He already knew she had a caring side to her nature. That was a possible plus. She seemed to enjoy silly chat, though. But maybe she just had the ability to adapt to the company she was in. That, too, could be good. How did she act towards her employers? He'd soon see; Martyn Edmunds had just joined the group.

'Hey, you lot,' said Martyn. 'You're supposed to circulate. Charm the passengers to make sure they keep flying the Edmunds' way.'

'Right, Captain,' said Garry. 'I'll go and tell that blonde bombshell over there all about what makes Dorniers tick.'

As the others made haste to follow Garry's example and circulate, Martyn drew Annie to one side. 'Are you all right, pet?' he asked as, hands on her shoulders, he held her at arms' length and ran a professional eye over her.

'I'm fine, Martyn. Really I am.' She knew the physical and mental wellbeing of his staff was of the utmost importance to him.

'You certainly look terrific,' he said. 'Was it sensible to wear such high heels, though?'

'I don't think they're causing any problems. Look.' Playfully she lifted her calf-length dress higher and stuck one leg out in the air.

It was then she felt the tingle run down her spine. But surely *he* couldn't be here. Could he?

Catching her breath, she lowered both dress and leg and, trying to act with a nonchalance she was far from feeling, slowly turned her head as if to casually survey the crowded room.

It wasn't so much his height that made him stand out from the rest of the crowd, more the aggressive male sensuality that seemed to emanate from him. And the silent sadness was there, too, tugging at her senses.

Though why Gail and Martyn should have invited an Air Ministry official to the party was beyond her comprehension.

'Annie?' Somewhat bewilderedly, Annie became aware of an alien voice. For a few seconds — minutes, hours? — everyone except the man lounging against the pillar had ceased to exist; it had been as though they were alone together.

'Oh, Gail. Sorry, I didn't see you. Did you say something?' To Annie's ears, her voice sounded husky, but if Gail noticed she didn't comment on it.

In fact, for the second time that day, Gail appeared to be flustered.

'We'll go over and I'll introduce you to him.' There was no need for Annie to ask to whom. Gail was looking in his direction as she spoke.

'I'll pass on that one, thanks all the same, Gail.'

'I know he wants to talk to you, Annie. I told him this afternoon I'd try and find an opportune moment.'

'He's got legs, hasn't he?' *Long, sexy legs.* 'If he wants to talk to me, all he has to do is put one foot in front of the other and — '

'I think he wants to see you alone.'

A pulsing knot formed in Annie's stomach. She knew she was attracted to him. She didn't want to be. She didn't want to feel anything for any man ever again. Best not to talk to him.

'Please, Annie. It's to do with . . . with our future plans,' said Gail.

'He could be quite important to them,' Martyn said.

Annie nibbled her lower lip. So it was work-related. Well, of course it was. Why else would he want to talk to her? He probably wanted to see if he thought she was responsible enough to be a flight attendant.

Hildy's joking words from that morning came to mind. But, Annie told herself, surely she wouldn't be thought unsuitable because of the slight friction there'd been between her and the official when they'd had words in the middle of the road?

Though she'd always thought A.M. officials checked over planes, not people. Knowing his reason for wanting to talk to her wouldn't make it any easier. But if it would help Gail and Martyn and the airline's future . . .

Gail touched Annie's arm. 'So?'

'OK. Lead me into the lion's den,' Annie replied reluctantly.

'You won't be . . . ?' Gail looked pleadingly at Annie. 'I mean, you will try to be nice to him?'

'Annie's nice to everyone.' Martyn spoke jovially, but Annie sensed that he was anxious too, and hastened to put his and Gail's minds at rest.

'Don't worry. I'll be on my best behaviour.'

'That's settled then.' Gail hooked her hand through Annie's arm and then glanced at her husband. 'Martyn, Violet's over there.' Gail indicated Edmunds' oldest passenger: a sweet, and rather large, independent nonagenarian.

'I'll go and have a few words with

her,' said Martyn.

'Lucky Martyn,' Annie said, as Martyn walked off.

Gail laughed. 'Violet will be on your flight tomorrow, you can talk to her then. Now, come on,' she added, with a gentle tug on Annie's arm.

A noisy group had arrived at the bar. Circling round them, Gail said, 'Listen, Annie, it's all right for you to answer anything he might ask about Edmunds'. Anything at all.'

Annie nodded. But she wished she wasn't the one having to do PR work on the Ministry official. And what could she tell him anyway? She didn't know what Gail and Martyn's expansion plans were.

But the main thing worrying her, she admitted, glancing up the length of the man leaning against the pillar and feeling that magnetic pull again, was whether she could cope with spending time with the man who oozed chemistry from every pore.

After performing the introduction, 'Zak,

this is Annie Layton; Annie . . . Zak Hunter,' Gail tactfully excused herself, leaving Annie feeling as though she'd been left in a canoe without a paddle.

Zak Hunter. The name suited him, went with his face: a rugged face, all chiselled angles, a wide but firm mouth. Unsmiling, Annie noted; then felt the heat rise in her face as she realised she was wondering how his lips would feel and taste. He had a square chin with almost a dimple in the centre, and . . .

'You seem to be on very friendly terms with Gail's husband?'

Even when he was apparently criticising, his voice still contained a plangent timbre. Suddenly, Annie felt annoyed. Annoyed by what he'd said, or annoyed at the way his voice affected her? She uncurled her toes, looked up into his dark eyes, and saw, not condemnation, but . . . But what? Pain? Regret?

Then he groaned and shook his head. 'I'm sorry. That remark was uncalled for.'

'I can see how it might have looked to

an outsider,' Annie said. 'Martyn's like
. . . like a father figure. Not just to me
but to all his staff . . . female and male.'

'A very diplomatic reply, Miss Layton.'

'Diplomacy can be a flight attendant's best friend, Mr Hunter.'

To her surprise, he laughed, revealing
a perfect set of white, even teeth.

Annie felt her own lips twitching in
sympathy. But Hildy had been right.
This man was dangerous. Zak Hunter
was all male; a raw, full-blooded male.
One who created havoc with her libido.

His laughter tailed off and, as their
eyes met again, an arc of awareness
flashed between them. It was no good
pretending it wasn't there. No matter
how much she didn't want it to be, it
really was. *With bells on*.

To cover her confusion, Annie lowered her gaze and tried to concentrate
on his clothes. An immaculately-cut suit
— cashmere, if she wasn't mistaken — and
his soft grey tie and pastel-striped shirt
were surely silk?

Her fingers tingled as she imagined

running her hands over his shirt to feel for herself the hard muscular chest she was sure lay underneath the silk covering. How she'd like to . . .

'Well, would you like to?'

Startled, she jerked her head up. He hadn't read her mind, had he? And how *could* she have been thinking such thoughts, anyway? She was off men. 'Er . . . s-sorry,' she stuttered. 'I didn't hear the question. Would I like to what?'

For a moment, Zak found himself unable to repeat his question. He was lost in the beauty of her dove-grey eyes. She had the cutest nose with a slight sprinkling of freckles, there was a soft colour in her sweet curved lips, and her chin . . .

Darn it all. He was meant to be taking a professional interest, not behaving like a lovelorn teenager. And she was waiting for him to answer.

He cleared his throat. 'Would you like to come and choose something from the buffet, and then we can find a quiet corner where we can eat and talk?'

Being in a quiet corner with Zak Hunter was the last thing she wanted. But Gail had asked her to be nice to the man, and to answer any questions about Edmunds'. As yet, he hadn't mentioned the airline.

'OK,' she replied. 'That's if we can find our way through the crowd to the buffet table.'

'No problem,' he assured her. 'Follow me.'

And of course, she thought, half-admiringly and half-crossly, as she followed meekly in his wake, he's got the commanding sort of presence that compels people to make way for him.

She'd no doubt at all that Zak would find a corner, too. Ready and waiting for them — and them alone — to ensconce themselves in.

'Did you hang a reserved sign on the plant?' she asked when, with a delicious-looking selection of food, he led the way to an empty and secluded spot. Well, empty apart from the huge Brugmansia plant with its orange trumpet flowers filling the air around them with a heady scent.

Zak looked at her with a blank expression. So, all right, she didn't score points when it came to being *funny* funny, but he could have tried to smile.

'Careful planning can be one of *my* best friends.' He parodied her earlier words; now the beginning of a smile tipped the corners of his mouth, and the hint of crinkle lines appeared at the corners of his eyes, softening his granite-like face.

Cripes. Annie swallowed. *I know I'm off men, but . . .*

There was a soft colour on her cheeks in her sweet curled lips; one delicate wrist was raised as she twirled a tendril of hair around her finger; her neck looked warm and shapely, and the soft material of her greeny-grey dress swept gently over her curves. Zak wanted to hold her, wanted to bury his face in her hair . . .

But he wasn't here to judge her femininity.

'Hold these.' He pushed the loaded plates towards her. 'I'll go and get us a drink.'

What would you like, Annie? she said inside her head. *Something long and cool? Alcoholic or non-alcoholic?*

Nevertheless, in spite of being annoyed at the way he'd neglected to ask, she feasted her eyes on his back view for as long as she could see it. It was well worth looking at.

And thinking like that, she reminded herself, is the path to unhappiness. She started to tick off in her mind all the things she *didn't* like about him. No manners. He was as changeable as a weathercock; he made caustic remarks; one minute he seemed to be warming up, the next he was as cold as a frog.

Ah, but when you kiss a frog . . .

Stop that, Annie. She took a deep breath and tightened her lips.

Then she became aware of Martyn standing in front of her.

'It's OK,' she assured him, noting his worried look. 'I haven't sent Mr Hunter off with a flea in his ear, he's — '

'Listen,' Martyn interrupted urgently, 'I think there's something wrong with Violet. She didn't seem at all her usual chirpy self when I was talking to her. Then she excused herself to 'go and powder her nose'. That was a good ten minutes ago, and now I can't see her anywhere.'

Annie thrust the plates of food into his hands; then, with a determination that outdid even Zak's, she made her way unhindered to the door and hurried down the hallway to the Ladies'.

Violet was sitting on a pink padded stool in front of the mirror, her veined hands pressed against her stomach, her handbag open on her lap.

'Tummy-ache, Violet?' Annie asked in a soothing manner. Her first-aid training came to the fore, as her gentle fingers noted the fast pulse rate and her eyes registered the fear in the old lady's face.

'Have you been sick, sweetheart?' she queried calmly. And, at Violet's nod, continued in the same calm manner, 'Is your cloakroom ticket in your bag? May I look for it?'

'In the small pocket at the front,' Violet murmured.

Annie found the ticket. 'Well, just stay where you are. I'll be back in a second, I promise. I'm just going to find someone to fetch your coat.' And someone else to drive us to hospital, she added silently.

It came as no surprise to Annie when, on opening the door, the first person she saw was Zak. She guessed Martyn must have told him she'd come to check on Violet. In spite of having made that mental list of what she didn't like about Zak, he'd shown before that he could be kind and thoughtful if he thought someone needed help.

'We need to get Violet to hospital,' she said quietly. 'Will you bring your car right up to the door? She'd hate being taken out on a stretcher, and anyway, it'll be quicker this way.' She didn't doubt for a second that, wherever he'd parked his car, he'd be able to get it out.

A quick look back over her shoulder at Violet told her there was no time to waste in sending anyone for her coat. But maybe Zak had a jacket or something in the car.

To Annie's relief, just as she was helping Violet to her feet, Hildy hurried in.

'Martyn sent me,' said Hildy. 'He's looking for Gail,' she added, going to Violet's other side.

'All right, Violet,' Annie explained, 'Hildy and I are going to basket-chair you outside to a nice warm car. Don't worry, we've done this before.' Then, catching Hildy's glance, Annie's mouth formed the words, 'Could be her appendix,' before lowering her head to talk softly to the frightened old lady.

For Violet's sake, Annie was relieved that they didn't see a soul as they made their way through the hallway and the entrance hall.

As if by magic, the front door swung

open just as they reached it, and there was Zak with a travelling rug over one arm.

After wrapping it deftly around Violet, he carefully lifted her into his arms and whispered something that caused a weak smile to form on her lined face. Then he moved smoothly away and down the steps.

As though his burden was as light as a newborn baby instead of the one hundred kilograms Violet had once ruefully admitted to, thought Annie, as she nipped past them to Zak's car.

The door to the back seat was open and Zak had left the engine running, Annie observed, as she slipped across the seat and held out her arms ready for Violet.

'What shall I tell Garry?' asked Hildy as she leaned into the car to help settle Violet comfortably.

Zak, already sliding into the driving seat, replied before Annie had a chance to. 'Tell him I'll see Annie safely home.'

3

It was past midnight when Zak and Annie finally left Violet tucked up in a hospital bed, awaiting an operation to remove her appendix. It had taken skill and guile to placate the old lady; worrying her more than the thought of an operation had been the knowledge that she'd be unable to deliver her great-grandson's birthday present.

'It's the first birthday he'll have had in Amsterdam,' Violet had tearfully told Anne, time and time again. 'That's why I was booked onto tomorrow's flight. I was taking him a giant teddy-bear.'

'Your grandson always meets you at the airport, doesn't he, Violet? Well listen, sweetheart: you tell me where you've put the teddy, and I'll get it for you when I fetch your nightie and all your other bits and pieces from your flat. I'll take Mr Ted with me tomorrow, and when we land I'll go and find your grandson, tell him you're not too well and give him the bear to take home for the little one.

'I'll recognise your grandson — you've often shown me the photos of your family, remember — and I'll tell him there's no need to worry about you,' she'd added, guessing that would be Violet's next concern. 'So you stop worrying about everything, let the doctors look after you and get rid of your pain, and I'll see you tomorrow.'

'Violet's grandson won't be at the airport,' Zak said as he and Annie made their way back to his car. 'He's her next of kin, the hospital have already phoned to tell him Violet's here.'

'I made a couple of phone calls myself, while you were talking to the doctor when we first arrived. One to Martyn to okay my idea, and one to Violet's family to put the said idea into action.' Annie smiled up at him. 'Edmunds' is flying the family over tomorrow. Great-grandson included. Violet will still get to see him on his birthday after all. But,' she added, 'I didn't dare tell her, just in case it made her think her family coming meant she was dangerously ill.'

'You're one heck of a lady, do you know that?' Zak said huskily, his lips close to her ear as he stretched across her to unlock the car door.

'A hungry lady,' Annie quipped. 'My tummy's rumbling.' And turning somersaults because of Zak's proximity, she realised.

As she settled back in the comfortable seat, she had to fight against the urge to put her hand to her ear and touch the place Zak's lips had brushed.

'You aren't the only one who's hungry,' Zak said, as he got into the car and started it up. 'But it's taken care of. I made a phone call, too. I've booked a table at *Pied a Terre*. It won't matter that it's so late, the owners know me quite well. I always eat there when I'm in the area.'

'It'll make you later still if you drive me home first,' Annie said. 'My house is in the opposite direction from *Pied a Terre*. If you pull in at the next lay-by, I'll phone for a taxi to pick me up from there. I needn't go to collect Violet's things yet; I'll go and fetch them in the morning, she won't need them until then.'

'What are you talking about?' Zak flicked her an amused glance. 'Why should I tell you I've booked a table if I hadn't booked it for two?'

Annie bit hard on her lip and shook her head. She'd have liked nothing better than to share a meal with the man beside her, and what could be a more natural conclusion to the evening after everything that had happened? But shadows of the not-so-distant past still lived in her mind and she felt wary.

For heaven's sake, she told herself rigorously, I won't set eyes on Zak again after tonight, and he's only suggesting a meal.

In that uncanny way he had of appearing to read her thoughts, he snapped, 'I'm not suggesting anything other than a meal, if that's what's worrying you.'

'It's not that . . . I mean . . . ' Annie floundered and then asked the question she'd been longing to ask all evening. 'I mean . . . are you married or attached in any way?'

'That would bother you?'

'Yes, it would,' she replied baldly. 'Even though we both know you'd only be feeding me, you said you always eat at the restaurant when you're in the area. It is after midnight and the restaurant owners might think — '

'You can rest assured,' Zak said, 'that if I were married or attached in any way, I'd have ordered you a taxi to take you home from the hospital. Satisfied?'

'I suppose so,' Annie said, trying to ignore the warm glow flowing through her.

'Is that a 'Thank you, Zak, I'll be glad to join you for a meal'?' he asked.

She chuckled throatily before answering. 'Thank you, Zak, I'd love to join you for . . . ' Her mouth dried and her tongue stuck to the roof of it.

Tarnation. Think food. Think eating.

'I'd love to join you for a meal,' she gabbled. 'I've never been to that French restaurant, it's reputed to be the best in Suffolk.'

Zak nodded. He felt powerless to say anything. That throaty chuckle, the small break in her voice, had been so . . . He shuffled slightly in his seat. *Brain to body. This is business.*

He forced himself to keep that in mind for the next ten minutes. He could smell Annie's perfume — something lightly floral and enticing. She wasn't sitting close, but he was still aware of the gentle rise and fall of her shoulder as she breathed. Aware of her delightful ankles and her high-heeled shoes . . .

'You've just driven past the restaurant's car park,' Annie said helpfully.

'I always park at the back.' Zak turned onto the small road at the side of the restaurant and hoped to goodness there *was* somewhere to park

48

behind it. The quicker they were out of the car, the better.

* * *

It seemed to Annie that Zak had understated things when he'd told her that the owners of the restaurant knew him quite well. They greeted him like a very old friend and with anxious enquiries as to how the old lady was.

He must have told them about Violet when he phoned, Annie thought. Yes, they know each other more than just quite well. This fact was further borne out when she saw that the door was locked and the 'Closed' notice displayed. Then Annie and Zak were ordered to take their time over choosing their food.

'My husband and I haven't had our own meal yet,' the attractive middle-aged woman informed Annie. 'After we've served you, we'll eat in the back and leave you to talk privately, yes?'

'Yes. Thank you, Colette,' Zak answered

49

warmly as he led Annie over to a small table set in an alcove.

A vase of lilies-of-the-valley welcomed them. 'Scented ones in October!' said Annie, sniffing in delight.

'We force them to grow indoors through autumn and winter,' Colette explained. 'I'll remove them when your meal is served. Their fragrance interferes with the food's aroma. But you'll get to take them home,' she promised with a smile. 'Perhaps you'll press and dry them to save as a happy memento, yes?'

Thankfully, Colette didn't wait for an answer. Instead, she placed the menu in Annie's hands, and Annie busied herself by reading it. Nevertheless, she knew that was exactly what she would do with the flowers.

Then she had to hide a smile as Colette gave a sharp order: 'Bert, the wine, bring the wine.' It seemed so incongruous somehow, to hear the jolly little Frenchman called by such an English-sounding name.

'*Albert, probablement,*' Zak whispered with an exaggerated and appalling French accent, and Annie giggled delightedly.

She just couldn't get used to all the different facets that were part of this man. But never, Annie realised thoughtfully, never did the soulless look quite disappear from his dark eyes.

Once again, she wondered if he'd had some recent tragedy in his life. And once again, he caught her with wandering thoughts as he asked if she'd had enough time to decide what she wanted to eat.

'*Soupe l'oignon gratinée* followed by *Ailes de raie aux câpres,*' she said quickly.

Then pleasure coiled through her as Zak laughed and said, 'My choice exactly.' It was hard to believe they'd both chosen the same dishes from the comprehensive menu.

Unless this was yet another side to Zak? Maybe he didn't want to put Colette and Bert to a lot of trouble at this time of night.

But, no, it wasn't that at all; for, with

a mock sigh, Colette stated: 'Always this man he has the same to eat. Onion soup with cheese, followed by skate wing with capers.'

'Not forgetting *Mousse au Chocolate aux Noisettes et au Whiskey*,' Zak intoned solemnly.

'He has a weakness for chocolate. Even with *Baba au Rhum*, he once demanded a chocolate sauce!' And, shaking her head, Colette hurried away from the table.

'You'd love the Illicit Affair then,' Annie said, speaking mainly to cover the sudden shyness she unaccountably felt now they were alone again. 'It's a really wicked dessert, and *sooo* chocolatey.'

The sudden frown that appeared between Zak's dark brows puzzled her. 'In that case, I think it probably deserves a more congenial name,' he said. 'Now, tell me about Edmunds', Annie. How long have you been there?'

The pang of disappointment at those words was so sharp she had to stop herself from sighing aloud. So that was why he'd brought her here, to find out what he didn't have time to discover at the party. This wasn't a 'getting to know each other' occasion, it was work.

You shouldn't want it to be anything else, mocked her inner voice. You're off men, remember. They take you, use you, then hurt you and leave you to pick up the pieces.

Stop that. Just answer him, Annie.

Her voice sounded tight and cold in her own ears as she spoke as if reading from part of her curriculum vitae: 'I've been with Gail and Martyn since they started the airline five years ago. We started off with one Dornier and two flights a day. Amsterdam and London. Then after eighteen months we got another plane, and added another route between London and Manchester.'

Go, Annie. You're in the swing of it now.

'I was a sort of Girl Friday at first, I worked in admin; on Reception; I helped choose staff . . . ' She shook her head. 'Not the pilots or engineers . . . mainly the female staff. I cleaned the planes, and I even took over the catering when the caterer went on holiday.'

She paused, wondering if Zak wanted to make any comment. It seemed he didn't, so she went on, 'We're like one big family, and I include our passengers in that. Most of them are regulars, like Violet. That's all really, and here's our first course.'

They ate in silence for a while; then, after mopping round her dish with garlic bread, Annie said: 'Now it's your turn. Do you like working for the Air Ministry? It must give you a sense of power . . . refusing or issuing certificates and things.'

Glancing up, she caught a strange look on his face. Oh lord, she thought, he must think I had an ulterior motive in mentioning his job and certificates. Gail should have done the PR bit herself; she wouldn't have been so crass.

'I thoroughly enjoy my work,' he stated inscrutably. 'But back to yours, Annie. At what point did you become a flight attendant?'

'Two years ago,' she replied with equal brevity.

Zak waited until their main course was placed in front of them, then: 'Why did it take three years?'

He saw her wonderful eyes cloud mistily, then she looked down and the fringe of her lashes cast shadows on her cheeks. 'Annie?' He spoke gently. 'Are you all right? I didn't mean to upset you.'

'It's OK. I just don't feel particularly proud of myself when I remember what I was like at eighteen. My parents were killed in a plane crash, and I turned into a 'poor little me' person. If I wasn't busy feeling sorry for myself, I was busy biting everybody's heads off. I just felt so *angry*.'

She glanced up at him with a rueful smile. 'I was totally pathetic.'

'You were left alone, no other family?'

'I've got a sister, four years older than

me, but she was working away at the time. Oh, only in London, she came back for the funeral and everything; but afterwards, she just picked up her life. It didn't affect Katie as badly. At least, not outwardly. *That* made me angry, too.'

Annie shrugged and shook her head. Nothing seemed to affect her sister much. Katie hadn't seemed at all upset when her marriage broke down after only a few months. She'd shrugged it off, saying they were both too young to be tied down.

'But you?' Zak prompted, interrupting Annie's thoughts.

'I mooned around like a broken puppet for a year. Then Gail and Martyn forced me into working with them. They'd known my parents for years. I told you earlier Martyn was a kind of father figure to us all.'

Zak nodded.

'Well,' Annie continued, 'in a way, he and Gail became my substitute parents. Once I was working with them, they never pushed me into becoming a flight attendant. I couldn't bring myself to even set foot on a plane because of what had happened to my parents. But, because I'm so lacking in height . . . ' Annie managed a grin. ' . . . they'd earmarked me for one from the word go.

'Anyway, I eventually overcame my fear of flying . . . I went on a training course, and . . . ' Her smile seemed more natural this time. ' . . . and Cinderella got to go to the ball. That's what it felt like, becoming a flight attendant. But,' she added seriously, 'it sometimes scares me when I think back to the way I'd been before all that.'

'It's quite usual, you know, feeling the way you did,' Zak said. 'I've been there, done that. In fact — '

'Are your parents dead, too?' Annie asked sympathetically.

'Yes, but it was a long time ago. That doesn't hurt so much now.'

'Someone else . . . recently?'

'My youngest sister. Oh, she isn't dead,' he added quickly. 'But she so easily could have been.' He picked up his glass and had a long drink of water before continuing.

'Vicky was a surprise baby, born when my parents thought the family was complete; she was only four when they died in a car crash. My other sister, Emily, was nearly sixteen. I was nineteen, and I managed to keep the family together with the help of a marvellous housekeeper.

'Vicky always looked to me to solve her problems. That didn't stop after she married. It was more so, really, when she and her husband moved down here from Cumbria. She'd lived in Alston all her life, so it was a big change for her.

'Anyway, last week, she needed my advice and decided to come and see me. She was upset and shouldn't have been driving. Her car went off the road and hit a tree.'

'Was she badly hurt?' Annie asked.

'A long, deep gash on her face; bumps and bruises; and a couple of broken ribs. The cut will probably leave a scar, and that will lower her self-confidence even more. But, as I said, she could have been killed. And I know one thing, Annie. If I ever find the person who caused Vicky's unhappiness, I'll . . . I'll . . . '

He shook his head, drew in a ragged breath, and then picked up his knife and fork. OK, maybe he was overreacting — even if he found the person, it wouldn't make any difference to Vicky; wouldn't put things right for her.

It was the thought she *could* have lost her life in a car crash like their parents had — knowing what it was like living through the heartache, realising he might have had to live through it again — that was getting to him the most.

Annie speared a piece of food onto her fork and popped it into her mouth. She sensed that Zak was regretting telling her so much.

After the short, uneasy silence, she tried to lighten the atmosphere. 'I hope some Neighbourhood Watch person won't think I'm breaking in when I go to Violet's flat tomorrow,' she said brightly. 'I'd hate to be arrested for stealing a giant teddy-bear.'

'Another flight attendant's best friend?' Zak quirked an eyebrow.

'What? A giant teddy-bear?'

'I meant having the ability to completely change the subject. And you knew it.'

Annie grinned. 'Did I?'

Her smile faded as their eyes locked and held. Once again there was static in the air, an awareness full of dangerous possibilities.

Then Colette arrived to remove their plates. Annie swallowed a sigh. She felt . . . *Like a balloon must feel when someone bursts it.*

'Annie, do you mind if we forget the sweet and coffee?' She heard Zak's voice, his husky voice, as if it were coming from a long way off.

She shook her head.

Pushing back his chair, he stood up. 'I'll just go through and tell Colette and Bert,' he said.

Annie watched him make his way past the empty tables towards the back room. *Get a grip on reality, Annie. You're off men, and you've never been into a one-night-only relationship.*

When he came back to the table, she stood up and he silently handed her the lilies-of-the-valley. 'Oh, I'd forgotten Colette said she'd give me them to take home,' Annie said softly. It would be nice to have something to remind her of Zak.

* * *

Once Annie had given the directions Zak asked for, another uneasy silence surrounded them. Annie searched her mind for something to say. *Got it.* 'What make of car is this, Zak?'

'A Bristol,' he replied tersely.

Annie persevered, 'Bristol of Filton? Didn't they make aeroplanes as well at one time?'

'That side of the business was taken over way back. There have been several mergers since then. But I worked at Bristol Cars for a couple of years. I have great respect for the firm, which is why I chose to have this car.'

'You worked there? Are you an engineer as well, then?'

'Yes, and I've also got my pilot's licence. Talking of flying, how will you cope with your duties tomorrow on so little sleep?'

'It's not exactly a long and strenuous flight, Zak. But I'll hula-hoop for ten minutes longer than usual when I get up. Then I'll have a pick-me-up bath with essential oils in.'

'Rosemary and geranium?' he asked, surprising her. 'Vicky uses them,' he added. 'You remind me a bit of her, Annie. She likes snails, too.'

'Snails?'

'Yes. As in, the snail you were moving to safety.' He glanced quickly at her, giving that almost-smile that made her heart beat faster. 'You looked so embarrassed, I pretended I thought you'd said you were moving a nail.'

Annie giggled. 'I told Hildy that if I'd known an Air Ministry official was about to drive along that stretch of road, and if the snail *had* been a nail, I'd — '

'You'd have left it there. Is that what you'd have done? Nobody likes officials very much, do they?' Without waiting for an answer he continued, 'What else do you do, apart from hula-hooping, to keep fit? Do you play squash or tennis?'

'I love tennis, but strictly as an observer.'

'Do you sit glued to the television during Wimbledon fortnight, or are you always on duty at the wrong times?'

'I was on holiday for those two weeks this year, and actually saw some matches for real.'

She'd replied without thinking, then the enormity of it struck her. It had been on Men's Finals Day that she discovered Russell Oliver, the man she'd been going out with for months, was married. He'd been furious when he thought the two of them might have been caught on camera.

And then he'd told her why: 'My wife will be watching television. If she sees me sitting next to you . . . '

Annie hadn't waited to hear any more. Full of horror, despair and disbelief, she'd got up and stumbled away. And, although she'd been totally and completely unaware that Russ was married — he'd told her he'd never married because he'd never found the right person — she'd hated herself for a long time after that fatal day when she'd learned the truth.

Now, she waited for the usual feelings of pain, guilt and humiliation . . . It was all there, but didn't feel *quite* as vivid as usual. Was she beginning to get over it?

'I enjoy tennis, too,' Zak said. 'Both watching and playing. Swimming's another love of mine.'

That explains his powerful muscles, Annie mused, mentally snatching at the diversion of her thoughts. And so lost was she in thoughts of Zak's muscles, she almost let him drive past the turning he needed to take to reach her house.

Once outside the house, Zak became cold and withdrawn again. He declined, extremely positively, when Annie offered him coffee, telling her he'd sit in the car and wait until she was safely indoors.

Hurt by his attitude, she thanked him formally for the meal and let herself out of the car; but took care not to squash her lilies-of-the-valley.

* * *

And that's that, she told herself later as, for the umpteenth time, she thumped her pillow, trying in vain to find comfort.

Like planes that pass in the sky . . . hello and goodbye . . . then both continuing on their separate ways, never to meet again.

4

'You're looking good, Violet,' Annie said as she pulled a chair closer to the bed. She hadn't been allowed to visit when she'd brought in the bits and pieces from Violet's flat on Thursday; this was the first time she'd seen the elderly lady since her operation.

Violet smiled. 'Could be because they let me eat proper food for the first time in days. Whatever anyone says about hospital meals, that Sunday lunch was delicious. But what about you? Are you enjoying being back at work? Are you sure it wasn't too soon?'

Annie shook her head. 'I was going mad being at home all day. I'd got to the stage where I was talking to the vacuum cleaner and the washing machine. Besides, what with Katie leaving, Gail and Martyn needed me.'

'So your sister's left? A bit sudden,

wasn't it? Where's she gone? You know I love hearing about other people's families.'

'Well, Katie is an actress really. She was just covering for me between jobs, and when she was offered a part in a pantomime, she had to go straight away.'

It wasn't quite the truth, but it was near enough. 'She's in Bournemouth now, rehearsing. She phoned this morning to tell me about it.'

'I thought you seemed a bit down in the dumps. Are you missing her?'

Annie sighed. 'We were never close. So I'm not really missing her. I suppose I miss what might have been. But Katie was never what I'd call family-minded even when our parents were alive. She even got married without telling us.'

'Your sister's married?' Violet looked surprised.

'She *was*, that was five or six years back. It only lasted a few months.'

'So, if it isn't your sister, what *is* bothering you?'

'Nothing really. I just feel a bit . . . I don't know . . . a bit unsettled.'

'Well, where's that charming man of yours? I want to thank him for being so kind and gentle to me the other night.'

'He isn't mine, Violet. I hardly know him. That was the first time I'd met him. Well, second time really.' And she made the old lady chuckle with delight when she told her about her first meeting with Zak.

'Of course, I didn't know then that he was an Air Ministry official on his way to Edmunds'.'

'He must hold a very important position,' declared Violet. 'That luxurious car, an expensive suit and a pure silk shirt. Oh, yes,' she nodded, 'I may have had tummy-ache, but that didn't affect my eyesight. I may be over ninety, but my heart still fluttered when I felt his hard chest against my cheek. His arms felt good, too,' she continued mischievously.

Annie stifled a groan.

Violet chuckled and, as Annie's eyes

snapped open, said, 'You tell him I'd like to see him, Annie. It'll give you an excuse to talk to him again. You'd like that, I'm sure,' she added artfully.

'He was just passing through, Violet; he came to do a job, and now that's done, he's gone. I'll probably never see him again. The Ministry will send a different official next time.'

'Ha. Nice try at sounding as if you aren't bothered. Your eyes gave you away, Annie. Such a bleak look in them when you said you'd probably never see him again. He *did* make your heart flutter.'

'OK, he's quite good-looking.' *Quite.* 'But he's just a man, Violet. One head, two arms and two legs, like any other man.' *A back of the neck which makes my fingers tingle, a mouth made for...*

'Well, I would like to thank him for his kindness,' Violet said again. 'Maybe I'll phone him, I'm sure I could get his number somehow. And, while I'm talking to him, it would be only natural for me to mention your name. You

69

know, to see how the wind blows.'

'Violet, you're incorrigible,' Annie protested laughingly. 'But I'll miss having you on my flights when you go to live with your grandson in Amsterdam. He told me all about it yesterday when he flew home.

'Still,' Annie bent over the old lady and kissed her wrinkled cheek, 'I'll have you one more time, and I think we should have a farewell party for you before you go.'

'Maybe he'll be at that party, too,' said Violet, as Annie walked away from her bed.

Annie turned and smiled, but the smile left her face once she was outside.

She was finding it hard to settle back into her job, she acknowledged as she drove homewards. There seemed to be a strange, almost secretive, air about Gail and Martyn — probably something to do with the expansion, though Gail hadn't mentioned it again.

Yes, that was why she was feeling out of sorts. She didn't know how the expansion would affect her: didn't know whether she'd be flying a new international route or a domestic one, or if Gail and Martyn would be taking on new flight attendants she'd have to train.

Her restlessness was nothing to do with Zak Hunter, she told herself later as she got ready for bed. How could it be? She scarcely knew the man. And she certainly didn't want him . . . or any man . . . in her life. She was going solo.

But before she got into bed, she lowered her face towards the lilies-of-the-valley on the bedside table and inhaled their sweet scent. She'd pressed some of the flowers. Maybe she should have pressed them all? Then she wouldn't have this reminder of him, wouldn't dream of him.

⋆　⋆　⋆

The next morning, a technical hitch delayed the Amsterdam flight. Annie strolled around the departure area reassuring the waiting passengers that the delay shouldn't be too long.

A little girl, clinging to a woman's hand, tugged Annie's blue uniform skirt. 'Mummy and me aren't coming on your plane, but my daddy is. He's going to bring me a Dutch dolly home.'

'That will be nice.' Annie bent down to reply to the child. 'Before you go, you'll have to ask Hildy, the lady behind that desk over there, what you can call your doll. Hildy's Dutch.'

'Maybe *you* could help me choose the doll?' Smiling suggestively, the child's father looked Annie up and down as she straightened up. 'One with beautiful chestnut hair, like yours. Where's the other redhead who works here, by the way?'

Annie was aware of the sudden tenseness in the man's wife, saw despair in her eyes, and her heart sank. This creep must be the man Katie had been seeing. 'She's left,' Annie said firmly. 'She was only taken on temporarily, and won't be coming back; she's moved out of the area.'

'She looked a bit like you — must be

the hair. How about my earlier request? Will you help me choose a doll for my daughter?'

'I'll be happy to give you a list of shops,' Annie replied pleasantly and, nodding politely, she moved away and went over to speak to Hildy.

As she did so, she caught sight of a tall, dark-haired figure disappearing into Gail's office. Dark hair with silver streaks. Heck, Zak Hunter didn't have the monopoly on silver-streaked hair. It could be anyone.

Nevertheless, Annie couldn't prevent herself from asking Hildy if she'd noticed who it was going into Gail's office.

'You're right, it was him,' Hildy told her, not having to mention any name. 'Didn't you feel his eyes on you when you were talking to the couple with the little girl?'

'I was too busy hiding my disgust at the way that obnoxious man was acting. Ugh. He gave me the shivers. It's going to be a real fun flight, I can tell you.

He's sure to be an Oswald.'

'A what?'

'An Oswald. A.k.a., an octopus. You know, nasty tentacles . . . ' Annie broke off as Hildy snorted.

Annie giggled. 'But I don't know why I'm laughing,' she said. 'You should have heard the way he was talking, his wife was really upset. I felt like putting my hands round his neck and strangling him. What is it with married men that they need to act like that?'

Hildy stretched across the desk to straighten some pamphlets. 'Are you sure you aren't overreacting, Annie?'

Annie shook her head. 'I don't think . . . ' She broke off when she saw Zak Hunter approaching.

'You're probably still feeling bruised because of what happened to you. You should forget about that Slimebag Oliver,' said Hildy, her words falling into one of those sudden silences which sometimes occur in a crowded place.

'Good morning to you, too,' Annie muttered under her breath as Zak walked past, making no acknowledgement other than a hard stare on his way by.

'Oh, well, sounds like we're in business,' she said, as an announcement came over the tannoy. 'See you later, Hildy.'

* * *

Annie was much too busy herding her passengers to the plane to dwell over-much on the way Zak had ignored her. No, not exactly ignored: he had stared at her . . . or through her.

She shrugged her puzzlement and resentment away, and got on with her job.

As well as having to cope with the octopus man, who was every bit as bad as she'd feared he would be, she also had to answer the persistent questions of one particular passenger. Not that Annie minded, but this passenger had been on her flight last week, on her first day back, and he'd asked similar questions then.

Maybe he's something to do with the expansion, Annie thought, as she ploughed down the aisle serving coffee. Fighting off the urge to pour boiling coffee over the octopus-man, she glanced up and met a sympathetic gaze.

Well, if he is going to become part of Edmunds', he'll be a nice addition, she decided. This view was strengthened when, though she was expecting another lot of questions as she poured his coffee, the man said, 'I congratulate you on your attitude towards that pest. Firm but polite, must take some doing.'

'Thankfully, we don't get too many like him,' Annie said quietly. Then smiled to herself as the questions started again.

'Are you taught how to deal with them or does it come naturally to you?'

Yes, she thought, as she replied: 'A bit of both, really.' Yes, I'm sure this man must have something to with Gail and Martyn's plans.

★ ★ ★

When Annie finally returned to base, Hildy told her Gail wanted to see her. 'She said to go straight through to her office and help yourself to coffee while you're waiting, she'll be with you in a few minutes.'

'OK, thanks Hildy.'

Freeing her hair from its neat chignon and combing it with her fingers, Annie walked into the office. Straight into the arms of Zak Hunter. 'Whoops.' She gasped, automatically clasping his upper arms. 'I . . . er . . . I didn't know you were here, Zak.'

Her voice sounded breathless and husky, and her heart was racing at the enforced proximity. A hot tide of sensation whirled through her as she felt her face colouring; her mouth was dry and she ran her tongue over her lips as she gazed up at him.

Heaven help him. She looked so adorable, so appealing. If he couldn't find a way to quash his feelings, he'd find it darned hard to stick to the agenda he'd decided on when . . . his heart twisted painfully . . . when he'd overheard the receptionist sympathising with Annie.

It had been a shock. He hadn't even felt the faintest suspicion when his sister had told him what she knew about the woman her husband had been seeing:

'She knew he was married, Zak, right from the start. Oliver told me that when he admitted to things. Said her knowing he was married proved it wasn't serious for either of them. I think he sometimes took her with him on his business trips to Amsterdam. I've found red hairs on his suit jacket more than once when he's been there.'

Zak knew Oliver, his brother-in-law, flew with Edmunds'. He wondered why he hadn't realised the truth earlier. But he hadn't. Not until he'd heard Hildy talking to Annie — heard his brother-in-law's name. Heard Hildy telling Annie to forget Oliver.

He remembered how, at the party, he'd questioned Annie about her friendliness with Martyn. At the time, he'd believed her explanation. Then today, before Hildy's unintentional revelation, he'd seen Annie flirting with a waiting passenger. And *he* was probably married, too. There'd been a woman and a child with him.

Flirting with a married man could lead to more. As it clearly had with Annie and his sister's husband.

The nightmare pictures went through Zak's head again: Vicky driving when she was upset because of her husband admitting that he'd been seeing someone; Vicky crashing the car. In his nightmare, Vicky was dead and he was going through the pain of losing someone again. And that was Annie's fault. She'd known Oliver was married. That's what Oliver had told Vicky.

To think he'd actually thought Annie a sympathetic and caring person. The way she'd been with Violet . . . and then, in the restaurant, he'd felt as though there was a special bond between them.

Well, he knew the truth now. He just had to make sure he remembered it. Standing close like this, feeling Annie's warmth, was not helping. He almost laughed aloud at that understatement.

He had his plan. He'd already started putting it into action. It was time to act on the next part of it.

He moved her firmly to one side. 'Can't stop, Annie. I'm late for an appointment.'

★   ★   ★

'Annie, I'm sorry I was so long.' Gail breezed into the office and over to the percolator. 'Ready for another coffee? We've got a lot of talking to do. But your cup's here. Clean. How come you didn't you pour yourself a drink?'

Because, Annie replied silently, after Zak hurried away I remembered the letter I'd pushed unopened into my bag that morning. Thinking it would take my mind off Zak Hunter, I decided to read it.

Her name and address on the envelope was typed. She'd had no idea who the letter was from. If she'd known that, she'd never have opened it.

It was from the man who'd used her, who'd hurt her. The man she'd dropped like a hot potato when she'd discovered the truth about him. He was missing her, and was sure by now she must be missing him. He needed to see her and would call round to her house next week. Maybe she could take Wednesday and Thursday off work? If not, he would just keep calling until he found her at home.

Huh. The letter had taken her mind off Zak Hunter all right.

'Annie. What's wrong? You look awful.'

'Headache.' Annie forced the word out as Gail bent over her. It wasn't a lie, either. Her head was pounding relentlessly as the words written in the letter echoed round and round inside it.

'We'll talk tomorrow. You need to get home and go to bed,' Gail said firmly. 'I think Zak Hunter's around somewhere with Martyn. I'll ask him to run you home. You're in no fit state to drive. And — '

'No,' Annie interrupted forcefully. 'No, Gail.' She made herself speak more calmly. 'It's all right. I'll get Garry to drive me home. I'd rather be with a friend, not a . . . not a stranger,' she concluded lamely. *Not someone she'd allowed to arouse feelings in her.* Someone who'd temporarily made her forget her resolutions. The letter had brought home to her just how important it was to stick to them.

'OK,' Gail said, frowning slightly as though she were aware of something she couldn't understand. 'I'll phone through and ask Garry to meet you by his car. Martyn or I will drive yours back for you later, and we'll pop in to make sure you're all right.'

'No, don't bother, Gail. I mean, yes, could you bring my car for me please, but don't call in. I just want to go to bed and sleep.' Annie knew she wouldn't sleep but she couldn't bear the thought of Gail and Martyn fussing round her. She needed to be alone.

'All right. But if you're not feeling better in the morning, you're to stay at home. Our talk will keep.'

'I'll be better,' Annie said, knowing full well that she wouldn't be.

* * *

But, to her surprise, when she woke the next morning, Annie did feel better. That was down to Garry.

When he'd brought her home last night, she'd shown him the letter. 'No problem, Pint-size,' he'd said. 'We'll both take Wednesday and Thursday off next week, and I'll stay here. If Slime-bag turns up, I'll sort him out once and for all.'

It was still something she didn't want to go through, she thought, as she showered and washed her hair. But at least she wouldn't have to go through it alone.

And now she could look forward to her chat with Gail. She felt sure it was something to do with the expansion. The Ministry must have approved things; that was why Zak had been at Edmunds' yesterday. To give the official go-ahead.

Even thinking of Zak didn't disturb her this morning. She just wanted to hear about Gail and Martyn's plans. She'd get to work early to make sure they had plenty of time to talk about them.

★   ★   ★

'Take a seat, Annie. You've no doubt guessed that this is about the expansion?'

Annie nodded.

'Well, for some time we've been wanting to put on northern routes: Teesside or Carlisle to London.'

'I should think that would be good business,' Annie said.

'Yes, but we couldn't raise enough

84

capital,' said Gail. 'Especially after the Dragon Rapide came up sooner than we'd bargained for. And we had to purchase it or lose it. Actually, Annie, to be honest, we were running into grave financial difficulties. Without an injection of capital we'd have been finished. We'd have lost everything.

'Oh, it's all right now,' she assured, when Annie gave a horrified gasp. 'At least, we *think* it's going to be all right.'

She held up her hands and crossed her fingers. 'We decided to bring a partner in, and for the last four months we've been working towards setting up a sister company which will be based in the Teesside area. Not far from Durham. There are strange boundaries up there,' she added. 'Yorkshire, Teesside and Cumbria all sort of merge into each other.'

'Never mind that,' said Annie, a flicker of hope and excitement curling through her. 'This new partner . . . Gail, am I right in thinking he's been watching and questioning me? Like, last week, and again yesterday, for instance?'

Gail smiled and nodded. 'I couldn't tell you who he really was,' she excused herself apologetically. 'Not until things were a bit more definite.'

'I understand,' said Annie, feeling glad that when the new partner had flown incognito on her Amsterdam flight she'd taken the time to answer his questions. 'Did all his questions mean that he's interested in me personally . . . I mean, in my working capacity?'

Martyn — who, unheard by Annie, had entered the office — moved forward from where he'd been leaning against the door. 'In fact, Annie, he's asked for you specifically. Seems adamant. He saw and studied your file some time ago, and agreed with Gail and me that you'd probably be the ideal person to take with him. That's why he's been watching you and talking to you — so he could be sure.

'Actually,' he continued, 'when we were talking over a few details yesterday, I got the feeling he'd back out if he didn't get you.' Martyn spoke jocularly, but Annie could sense his underlying worry.

'You'd be up there for a few months, Annie, starting from scratch, just like we did here,' said Gail.

'Only this time, *you'll* be the public face of the company, Annie, like Gail was — and is — here. You'll be responsible for marketing, employing staff, training flight attendants, personnel, admin and much more besides. But the salary will match the responsibility, and the whole thing could lead to a directorship for you.'

'Martyn,' chided his wife, 'you're talking as though Annie's accepted. That's not fair.'

'I wasn't talking like that to persuade you into accepting,' Martyn said earnestly. 'We don't want to force you into anything, Annie.'

Annie laughed. 'You don't have to force me. I volunteer,' she said. 'It'll be a challenge; that's just what I need in my life at the moment to . . . to take my mind off other things.'

'You must take time to think it over.' Gail nibbled worriedly at her lip. 'It would be quite an upheaval, you know, Annie. You'd have to decide what to do about your house here, whether to leave it empty or rent it out. There's a house up there that goes with the job, by the way. But you wouldn't know anyone in the area — '

'Wrong,' said Annie. 'Do you remember Geraldine? She and I went to school together, you must have met her. Well, when she got married, she moved to Newcastle. That isn't too far away from Durham; it's a lot closer than it is to Suffolk, anyway.'

'Do you really think you'd like to take it on, Annie?' asked Martyn. 'We'd be sad to lose you, of course, but you would be coming back. As Gail says, you must take time to think it over . . . but we have got an appointment with the solicitor this morning, and it would be nice to have this final detail sorted out.'

'Martyn, you're rushing her again,' Gail protested. 'Look, Annie, there's an hour and a half before take-off. Perhaps you'd like to read through the contract of employment and see what you think.'

'OK,' Annie said. 'I'll read and digest, but I've already decided. I've never felt so sure about anything before.'

And so sure was she that, after reading through the contract, she signed her name with a flourish and without a second thought. 'There.' She laughed. 'You two hurry up and sign it now, and then you can't back out of it.'

* * *

The rest of the week passed in a flash. On Sunday evening after visiting Violet, who'd been moved to a convalescent home, Annie hummed happily as she drove to Gail and Martyn's house for a meal planned especially to celebrate her forthcoming role.

The new partner was coming; she was looking forward to meeting him properly. 'Though he must feel that he knows me inside-out after all the questions he asked me.' She chuckled, drawing to a halt in the driveway. 'Well, I'll be able to ask *him* a few tonight.'

'Annie, good, you've arrived first.' Martyn hugged her before leading her into the lounge. 'Gail and I wanted this chance to warn you that there might be some pressure put on you tonight.'

'Pressure to take up your new duties almost immediately.' Gail sighed. 'Which, if you agree, will in turn put pressure on me. Or at least on my neck and shoulders. I'll have to take your Amsterdam flight until we appoint a new flight attendant.'

Annie grinned sympathetically as she accepted a glass of wine. Gail was a couple of inches over the ideal height to work in comfort on the Dorniers.

'Still, I dare say I'll survive,' said Gail. 'Ah, I heard a car pull up; go and open the front door, Martyn.'

'How soon is 'almost immediately'?' Annie asked Gail.

'Wednesday morning has been mooted. Could you cope?'

'I guess so.' Annie nodded. In fact, Wednesday sounded like an answer to a prayer. There'd be no need to involve Garry in sorting out her unwanted visitor now.

'I've decided against renting the house out,' she went on. 'It's half my sister's, remember, and she does sometimes stay there when she's between jobs. I've already organised for someone to go in a couple of times a week to keep an eye on everything; she'll not object to starting a bit sooner, I'm sure. And . . . '

Annie broke off suddenly; she felt the colour creeping up her neck and face, and her heart was hammering. She sank hastily onto the soft leather couch, putting her glass down on a nearby table in case she spilt wine from her trembling hand.

She'd recognised the deep brown voice greeting Martyn. Neither he nor Gail had mentioned the fact that Zak

Hunter would be here, too.

'We've warned Annie that you're going to try and persuade her to take up her new duties sooner than she'd expected to,' Martyn said as he walked back into the lounge with Zak.

Filled with disbelief, Annie waited in vain for a third person to come through the door. Martyn couldn't have been talking to Zak. He just couldn't have been.

But there was nobody behind Zak.

Annie clenched her hands so tightly she could feel her nails digging painfully into her palms. *No-o-o.* Even through her shock, she could feel that powerful magnetism again.

'Well, well, this really is an occasion; a big step forward, or should that be a steep flight upwards, for Edmunds' Airways. And it could be a real milestone in your life, Annie.' Seemingly unaware of the electric atmosphere, Martyn burbled happily away as he poured a glass of wine for Zak.

'A real milestone.' Zak repeated

Martyn's words. And he was nearer now, standing by the couch. She could feel his gaze on her and, against her will, she looked up to meet it.

'You told me you worked for the Ministry.' She spoke almost pleadingly, as if begging him to agree. He couldn't work for the Ministry and be a partner in Edmunds'.

'No.' He shook his head and gave that almost-smile. 'I told you I enjoyed my work. And something tells me,' he added, placing his glass of wine next to hers before sitting down beside her, 'that I'm going to enjoy it even more in the near future. I'm so happy you have agreed to come and work with me at our new base.'

Pointless for her to reply she hadn't known it was him she'd be working with; she didn't feel capable of speech anyway. Pointless for her to admit that she'd thought the new partner was the passenger on her flight who'd asked her all those questions.

Not that it mattered. What mattered

now was deciding whether she could work with this man whose virile strength was stamped into every line of him. Whose very presence made her insides feel like melting jelly.

But Zak was still talking, and Annie made herself look at him. 'I know, when you signed the contract . . . '

The contract. He must have known she'd no idea he was the new partner when she'd signed the thing. Maybe he'd warned Gail and Martyn not to mention his name. *Oh, for heaven's sake. Pull yourself together, Annie.*

She was reading this all wrong. OK, so he wasn't an A.M. official, but neither was he some sultan choosing a concubine, for heaven's sake. And if she tried to renege, he might back out; and, from what Gail had said, Edmunds' desperately needed him, or at least his cash injection.

She couldn't let Gail and Martyn down, just because she was scared of the way Zak Hunter made her feel. They meant too much to her. And anyway, surely she'd stop feeling attracted to him now she knew he had lied to her? Because, just like Slimebag had lied, Zak had been guilty of lying, too; by not denying it when he'd known she'd thought he worked for the Ministry.

Annie didn't think she'd allowed these thoughts to show on her face. She prayed her training had held her in good stead and, somehow, she'd managed to keep her gaze determinedly on his.

After a brief pause, Zak went on: 'I know the starting date on the contract was a month away, but I'm sure you'll see your way to accommodating us by agreeing to an earlier start.'

'No problem,' Annie said.

Zak reached for their wineglasses and gave Annie hers. 'And let's drink to 'no problems' in our new venture.'

As they clinked glasses, Annie wondered if she'd imagined the note of irony in Zak's voice.

5

'I think you're nuts if you go and work with him,' Hildy stated flatly.

Annie carried on building a house out of beer mats. Her thoughts over the last twenty-four hours had been similar to Hildy's.

She had hoped, when she'd arranged to meet Garry and Hildy for a farewell drink, that neither of them would bat an eyelid when she mentioned that the new partner wasn't the man who'd asked so many questions on her flight, but was Zak Hunter.

'What's wrong with it being Zak Hunter?' demanded Garry. 'Surely it doesn't make any difference *who* Annie is working for up there. It's still a feather in her cap to be chosen for the position. I mean — ' He turned to Annie and grinned. ' — I know you said you volunteered, but it was you they wanted.'

'When she volunteered, she thought she'd be working with someone else. Honestly, Garry, you haven't seen the way Zak Hunter stares at her. It's . . . ' Hildy fished the slice of lemon out of her gin and tonic, and sucked it thoughtfully. 'It's not very nice.'

'What? The lemon, or the way Zak Hunter stares at Annie? She's worth staring at, you know.'

'It isn't an M.A.W. look,' Hildy said.

'A *what*?' Annie and Garry queried together.

'A 'Man Admiring Woman' look. No. The way he looked at her that morning last week . . . you know, Annie, when the flight was delayed? Well, he looked . . . vengeful. Yes.' Hildy nodded firmly. 'That's the word I was looking for. Vengeful.'

'You've been reading too many thrillers,' Annie said.

'I'm serious, Annie. I think you should *unvolunteer* yourself, I really do.'

'Oh, yes.' Annie gave a wry smile. 'I

can just imagine how it would sound, telling Gail and Martyn that I've decided I can't take up my new post because of the way Zak Hunter looks at me. Anyway, I'll only be up there for a few months when all's said and done.'

Hildy shook her head. 'I still think you should back out of it.'

'I've signed a contract, remember? Besides . . . ' Annie bit her lip; there was no way she could explain that if she backed out of it, Zak might also back out; and that that would cause problems for Gail and Martyn. She was far too loyal to mention the fact that the airline had been in financial difficulties.

'Besides,' she continued firmly, 'I'm quite looking forward to the challenge. Now, that's enough of Zak Hunter for one night. This is supposed to be a party, not a wake. Whose round is it?'

And, determinedly, Annie led the conversation away from Zak Hunter, and they talked instead about the place in which she'd be living.

'According to Gail, the house which

goes with the job is on the outskirts of a village called Bowes, that's near Barnard Castle. It's quite a hilly area; I'll have to invest in some good walking boots. The only drawback I can see as yet is that it's about twenty miles away from base. Quite a long journey there and back every day.'

'Lucky after all that you listened to Uncle Garry, and traded in that old heap you had for a decent car.'

Unfortunately, Garry mentioning the car brought Zak Hunter firmly back to Annie's mind. She tried to swallow her anger as she remembered what he'd said last night, just before she'd left Gail and Martyn's house.

It had been decided that Gail would take over Annie's duties straight away. 'The least we can do is to give you tomorrow and Tuesday free to do all your packing.' Gail laughed ruefully. 'And two days is scarcely enough, but at least the house is fully equipped with everything you'll need. You are sure about that, aren't you, Zak?' she'd added.

'Fully-furnished and fully-equipped,' he assured. 'We'll leave early on Wednesday morning, Annie, to arrive before dark. Can you be ready by six o'clock? Then we can take an hour or so to pack whatever you want to take with you.'

'I'll load up my car the night before,' Annie replied. 'And there's no need for you to come round, Zak; I'll manage to find Bowes myself. I can follow a map, you know.'

'You don't need to bother about a map,' Zak said. 'You'll be travelling with me and I know the way.'

'Don't be ridiculous, I'll need my car up there.'

'Correction. You'll need transport, yes. But not yours, Annie. As far as I know, your particular make of car does not possess four-wheel-drive. And a four-wheel-drive is what you'll need. There's a suitable vehicle ready and waiting for you.'

'Think of the wear and tear you'll save on your car,' said Gail. 'It will still be like new after sitting in your garage for a few months.'

'Talking of garages . . . ' Zak said. 'Unfortunately, Annie, there isn't one at your new home, but I've managed to rent one for you a few minutes' walk away. You won't need to hula-hoop to keep in trim,' he added. 'You'll be taking a brisk walk every morning.'

'There, that's settled then.' Martyn had spoken into the tension-filled silence. 'You'll be travelling in comfort, Annie. You'll be able to sleep all the way if you feel like it, and be nice and fresh for work the following day.'

Zak nodded. 'Yes, I've arranged several meetings for Thursday. We'll also have to find time to go on site and see how the builders are progressing. So, as Martyn said, by travelling with me you'll have the added benefit of being nice and fresh for work.

'So.' He looked challengingly at Annie. 'You'll be ready with your cases packed at six o'clock Wednesday morning, then.'

It hadn't been a question and Annie

hadn't deigned to answer. Oh, she'd be ready all right. But her cases would be in her own car. And she'd drive at a steady thirty miles an hour all the way. Zak would soon get fed up with that and leave her to make her own way to Bowes . . .

'You still with us, Annie?' Hildy's plaintive voice brought Annie back to the present. 'Some farewell this is, when you don't even talk to us.'

'Sorry, Hildy. My mind does seem to keep wandering away. Tell you what, let's finish our drinks and go back to my place. I'll cook us a fantastic impromptu last supper.'

★   ★   ★

Annie spent most of the next day sorting out what to take with her. By early evening, she was loading her car.

Arms laden with a pile of books, and slightly off-balance, she stumbled as she took the two steps down from the kitchen into the garage. The top book slid off and landed on one toe, causing her to mutter a vehement curse.

'Tut-tut, such charming language.' The voice came out of the darkness from the direction of the open garage door, rendering Annie momentarily speechless.

However, she recovered quickly enough to counter, 'I thought you said six o'clock Wednesday morning, not six o'clock Tuesday evening?'

Making herself take the few paces needed to reach her car was harder. She felt as if her kneecaps were on back to front. She made it, though, and unceremoniously allowed the books to slither from her arms into the cardboard carton she'd placed in the car to receive them.

Then her breath caught in her throat as he uncoiled his lean length from the doorway and, with inherent animal grace, strolled towards her.

'What are you doing?' It was an entirely rhetorical question — it was quite obvious what she was doing, the cases and cartons were on full view in the back of the car.

'Painting my nails?' She gave a tentative smile.

Got no response.

The silence stretched between them as, hands thrust in the pockets of his soft leather jacket, he leant nonchalantly against the car.

His raw vibrancy struck her like an electrical charge; the storm-force potency of his personality, his magnetic draw, the faint scent of a woody male cologne . . .

She tried to throttle the dizzying current racing through her, tried to lower her gaze; wanted to move away, but his compelling ebony eyes riveted her to the spot.

Did he know that? Could he sense the unwanted feelings buzzing through her body like a swarm of demented bees? There was a maddening hint of arrogance about him, but his expression held a hint of amusement, too. Drat the man. This was so not fair.

She took a deep breath, squared her shoulders and broke eye contact.

Then . . .

'Have you got an electric blanket?'

Her gaze flew back to his face. 'E-electric blanket?'

'That's why I called in this evening, to tell you that I phoned my secretary and asked her to go round and double-check there was everything you needed in your new abode. She couldn't find an electric blanket, though there are a couple of hot-water bottles.'

'H-hot-water bottles?' parroted Annie.

'Yes. Surely you must have heard of such things? You fill them with hot water and they keep you warm.'

Annie moistened her lips.

'Of course,' he continued, 'there are other ways . . . '

'Just what is that supposed to mean?' flared Annie, appalled that he seemed to have read her unruly thoughts again.

The almost-smile she was beginning to recognise tipped the corners of his mouth. He pointed to the books in the carton. 'I was referring to your reading matter.'

She dragged her gaze away from his face and glanced down. It would have to be the romance novels that had landed cover-up, wouldn't it?

'They say,' he drawled, 'that the books a person reads can tell you a lot about that person. Though,' he added, almost to himself it seemed, 'I *thought* I knew what sort of person you were when I saw how gentle you were with Violet.'

'Violet.' Annie groaned. 'I'll be late for visiting now, thanks to you.'

'Surely not.' Zak shot back the cuff of his jacket and checked the time. 'It will only take you twenty minutes to get to the hospital.'

'Move out the way,' demanded Annie, reaching up to pull the hatch-back door down. 'Violet isn't at the hospital; she's in a convalescent home, an hour's drive away.'

'I'll come with you. We'll go in my car. Don't argue, Annie,' he commanded as she opened her mouth to do just that. 'It *is* my fault you're going to be late. I don't want you driving reck-lessly and having an accident. Besides, I'd like to see Violet again. And to make up for delaying you, I'll help you finish off loading up when we come back.'

'You're . . . you're not going to . . . ?'

'I promise I won't mention hot water bottles or romance novels.'

'I wasn't going to say that,' she said. 'I was just surprised about you offering to help me load up. I thought you'd still be insisting on driving me to Bowes tomorrow.'

Zak shrugged. 'One thing I do admire in a woman, and that's an independent spirit. Though in your case it's more a spirited independence. Now, are we going to see Violet or not?'

'Will you shut the garage doors for me while I grab my coat and bag?'

Zak nodded.

'I won't be long,' Annie said, moving speedily into the kitchen and relishing the thought of being free of his overwhelm-ing presence, if only for a few minutes.

What an enigma this man was. What

swaying emotions he caused within her, and what swaying emotions he seemed to possess.

She went into the hall, jerked her coat from the banister rail, picked up her bag and, with a vexed sigh, stared at the flowering tray she'd made for Violet. She'd left it on the small table, planning to take it upstairs to wrap. It was too late to do that now.

The hand she put out to pick up the tray halted in mid-air as Zak's voice came from behind. 'Allow me. Is it to come with us?'

'A present for Violet.' Annie winced inwardly as she realised how breathlessly she'd spoken. He'd startled her, that was all, she told herself. She'd expected him to lock the garage doors from the outside and to be waiting in his car for her.

Turning, she cast an anxious glance at him. Had he noticed her breathlessness?

Holding the tray in one hand, he lightly ran the forefinger of his other hand down her cheek. 'Cobweb,' he said succinctly, then stretched a long arm and used that same hand to open her front door. 'Come on, we'll never get there at this rate. And you'd better tell me exactly where it is we're going.'

She could still feel the touch of his finger on her cheek as she closed her front door behind them. But she'd no time to linger and savour it; Zak's long strides had already taken him through the gate and over to his car — already he was holding the passenger door open for her.

After listening to her concise directions, he glanced down to make sure she was wearing her seatbelt, then started the car without a word.

Occasionally, the headlights of other cars briefly lit up his dark hair. Hair that reminded her of a velvety midnight sky: a deep mysterious black, streaked in places with silver stardust. Only she wouldn't be able to glimpse those appealing streaks until he turned his head.

This was crazy. What did the colour of his hair matter? It could be bright green for all she cared.

But from under her eyelashes, she still watched, hoping that he'd look out of his window so she could see the back of his head.

When he did turn, while he'd pulled up at the traffic lights, it was towards her. 'Where did you buy that tray for Violet? I'd like to get two or three to serve drinks from on the planes.'

'I . . . ' She gnawed her lower lip. For some obscure reason she didn't want to tell him that she'd made the tray. Well, not the actual tray itself; she'd found that at a car-boot sale. Only then, it had been a badly-stained plain wooden one. Working with dried or pressed flowers was one of her favourite ways of relaxing. She loved turning plain or damaged objects into something beautiful.

'Do we turn right here?' he asked, saving her from having to answer his previous question.

'Yes, then immediately left, and the convalescent home is about three hundred yards down on the right-hand side.'

* * *

Violet was delighted to see them. For a while they chatted about the weather and food, the staff and the other patients, and then Annie told Violet that Zak was to be her new boss.

'You told me on Sunday you thought it was going to be the passenger on your flight who asked you all those questions.'

Annie nodded.

'It must have been a pleasant surprise for you, when you found out you were wrong.' Violet's eyes twinkled mischievously.

'I was also wrong in thinking it would be another couple of weeks before I moved up north,' said Annie. 'I'm going in the morning, Violet. This is my last visit.'

'Your last visit here, maybe. You'll be visiting me in Amsterdam. I don't need to tell you that the invitation comes from my grandson as well as from me.'

Violet turned her wrinkled face to Zak. 'Richard is full of admiration for Annie, you know. She'll be more than welcome in his home.'

'Does Richard's wife feel the same way, I wonder?'

Zak's tone may have been mild and inoffensive but, in the uneasy silence that followed the remark, Annie couldn't help but notice the look he turned on her. A cynical look, she told herself. Did that mean he'd heard she'd had a relationship with a married man? Had he got her down as a marriage-wrecker?

Or was she misreading Zak's expression, because anything that reminded her of what had happened brought back the sickly knot of despair in her stomach?

'Of course Richard's wife will welcome Annie!' said Violet. 'And as for my great-grandson . . . Well, he may only be three, but he's already stated his intentions of marrying her.'

'Now Zak can add cradle-snatching to my list of sins.' As Zak's had been, Annie's tone was also mild and inoffensive, but she knew her eyes were smarting with suppressed anger, and she was aware of her cheeks burning.

Zak faced her stonily and, to her secret disgust, she was the first to look away.

Her glance fell on the tray that Zak had unobtrusively placed by the side of Violet's chair. Grateful for the excuse to change the subject, Annie picked it up and handed it to Violet. 'I didn't have time to wrap it,' she apologised.

'Poppies and cornflowers, two of my favourites.' Violet's gnarled fingers wandered over the glass that protected the pressed flowers. 'It's beautiful, Annie, I'll think of you whenever I use it.'

'From the looks of things, you can use it straight away.' Zak waved a hand towards one of the attendants who'd arrived with a trolley of drinks. His voice was noticeably warmer this time.

It would be, of course, Annie thought painfully; those words had been for Violet alone and had held no hidden meaning.

'I guess it's time for us to go.' Annie got reluctantly to her feet; she wasn't looking forward to the journey home.

Bending swiftly, she embraced Violet and realised — as Violet returned the embrace and whispered, 'If you ever need a place to run to, you've got my address' — that the old lady hadn't been unaware of the unpleasant tension in the atmosphere.

And, Annie noticed, although Violet accepted Zak's farewell kiss, she didn't return it; and her 'Goodbye, thank you for coming' was decidedly cool.

*   *   *

Outside, a shy moon trembled palely above them, somehow enhancing the bitterness etched on Zak's face as he walked towards his car. His empty eyes seemed to stare right through her while, silently, he held the passenger door open.

Annie didn't know which was worse — the look he'd cast upon her before, or the empty stare she'd just received. Then anger and dismay at the knowledge that any sort of look from him could reduce her to such despair coiled through her, and she gazed steadfastly at the windscreen.

'I suppose I shouldn't have let my distaste for the way you behave show in front of Violet,' he said when he got into the car.

'The way I behave?' Annie's voice was hoarse with pent-up anger.

'What is it with you, Annie? Why do you have this predilection for married men? Don't you realise what hurt and anguish the innocent party suffers?'

So he did know about her past mistake. 'Don't you think I suffered hurt and anguish when I knew I'd been going out with a married man?' she said, her voice full of despair. 'I was the innocent party too, Zak. I didn't know he was married until we'd been seeing each other a while. The second I knew, it was over.'

Zak put his hands on the steering wheel and gripped it tightly. If Vicky hadn't told him her husband's mistress had known from the start that he was married, he would have believed Annie's anguish to be genuine.

'It was one man, one mistake,' Annie went on. 'You can hardly call that having a predilection — '

'No?' He turned his head to face her, and she shivered at what she saw in his expression. 'What about that character in the departure lounge . . . the one I saw flirting with you, in front of the woman and the little girl with him? They were probably his wife and child, but you chatted and smiled back at him. Then there's Violet's grandson, full of admiration for you and inviting you into his home. What about them, Annie?'

'For heaven's sake. I did my best to

let that passenger know his advances weren't welcome. And as for Violet's grandson, any invitation into his home would be for his grandmother's sake, not his. What is it with *you*, is more to the point. What right have you got to set yourself up as judge and jury?'

'I've seen the unhappiness caused when there are three people in a relationship,' said Zak with feeling.

'Were you once married, Zak? Were you unfaithful to your wife?' This explanation for his attitude towards her hit Annie like a bolt from the blue. The thought had entered her mind and been spoken instantaneously. Now she enlarged upon that thought.

'Is that what this is all about? Getting at me because of your own guilt? Well, I won't sit here and take it. I won't be condemned for other people's behaviour, Zak. I'm going to — '

She broke off with a gasp as his hands left the steering wheel to grasp her shoulders. 'You'll not back out of working for me, Annie.' His face was so close to hers she could see every pore; could see the faint, dark evening shadow on his cheeks.

'That could have serious repercussions for Gail and Martyn. Whatever else I may think about you, I know you're the right person to help set up the new base.'

'I wasn't going to suggest backing out. It would take more than a bitter twisted cynic like you to make me give up my new job. I was going to say, I'll take a taxi home and give you time to straighten yourself out.' She glared at him, wondering if she'd pushed him too far.

'No need for that.' He dropped his hands from her shoulders and watched as she put her own hands where his had been. He must have realised his grip had been painful, because he muttered an apology.

'I'm sorry. I didn't mean to hurt you; not like that, anyway.'

The last four words were spoken so softly that Annie wasn't really sure if she'd actually heard them. Wasn't really sure either if she should sit here meekly and allow him to drive her home. But he was starting the car now and she felt too weary to protest.

She felt sure that she'd discovered the reason for his outburst. She was sure he'd wrecked his own marriage by being unfaithful.

His marriage must have broken up quite recently for him still to feel so deeply. He obviously regretted what he'd done. Then there was his sister's accident, too. He'd made it clear that he felt vengeful towards the person who'd caused her accident. No wonder he was so bitter and cynical with all those emotions eating into his soul.

Whoa there. Annie caught herself up in dismay. She'd be feeling sorry for him if she carried on thinking that way. Whatever his emotions were, he'd no right to take them out on her. No right to make her a scapegoat for his wrongdoings. No right to put the blame on her for the way the octopus-man had behaved. And as for questioning the invitation from Violet's grandson . . .

She tried to bring back her anger, but a strange feeling of tenderness seemed to have taken its place. Tenderness, and a need to protect Zak from himself, from the hurt that was gnawing at him — destroying him.

Heck. What on earth was he thinking of, losing his cool and questioning her like that? Zak clenched his jaw so tight it sent shooting pains up his face. He'd always prided himself on his control, on not allowing his thoughts to show. Impassiveness was necessary, often a secret weapon, in business matters.

He must make sure he adhered to that in his dealings with Annie. He'd as good as told her he knew she had been his brother-in-law's 'other woman'. No way must he do that. Not yet.

He inhaled deeply. If she wasn't to suspect anything, he'd better start to repair any damage his outburst may have caused.

They travelled in silence for a few

miles before he said, 'Have you eaten, Annie?' He tried to speak casually, as if the unpleasantness had never taken place.

An olive branch? Annie wondered. OK, they were going to be working together; it would probably make things easier if she took his words as a sort of apology. Might make it easier for her to work on ridding him of his bitterness. 'No, but I've left a *Boeuf en Daube* simmering in the oven. You're welcome to share it.'

'Do you always cook enough for two, Annie, just in case of an unexpected guest?'

'Does that mean you accept?' Annie spoke sweetly, but inwardly she was fighting for composure. She'd just about had enough of his snide comments; her feelings of tenderness and protectiveness towards him were a nonsense. Why couldn't she just let him go ahead and destroy himself?

Because when Mum and Dad were killed, Gail and Martyn had been there for her. They'd stopped her from destroying herself with bitterness. She had to try and do something for Zak, even if she got hurt in the process. 'Seeing as you promised to help me finish loading my car,' Annie continued determinedly, 'the least I can do is offer you a meal.'

They were outside her house now. He drew to a halt, and in the glow from the street-light, Annie saw the look of bewilderment and indecision written on his face. Good. Maybe he was beginning to realise his boorish attitude wasn't getting to her.

She unsnapped her seatbelt and, without looking at him, got out of the car. Fingers mentally crossed, she opened the garden gate and left it open as though there were no doubt he'd follow behind.

★   ★   ★

Annie grimaced as the insistent shrilling of the alarm brought her rudely awake. She threw out a hand to switch the noise off and, although she knew she should get up, rolled onto her back to think.

It had been gone midnight when Zak left. There hadn't been any need for conversation when they'd packed the few remaining cartons into her car. Over the meal, however, she'd tried to find out something more about him.

He'd told her his home was an old farmhouse in Alston, and he had a live-in housekeeper. His sister Emily lived near him with her husband and two children. His secretary of two weeks was the daughter of good friends in Cotherstone. These friends owned the two houses he'd rented — one for Annie, and one where he'd live during the week so he could be close to the airfield. Zak also had another friend, Edward somebody-or-other, a veteran of the RAF, who would captain one of the crews.

That was it in a nutshell. Not much there, really. In fact, Zak had seemed to be in a thoughtful frame of mind. Annie smiled as she stretched and got out of bed. Maybe her calling him a bitter, twisted cynic had got through to him? Perhaps she'd see more of his sunny side and less of the dark savage complexities that lurked within him.

Annie continued her musings as she showered and dressed. Things would be much easier if Zak didn't snipe at her. If she could prevent his bitterness from creeping into their working relationship, it would make it easier for them to work in harmony. Maybe the harmony would continue outside working hours, too? *Get lost, Cupid. I don't want my heartstrings twanged.*

She hurried downstairs, went into the kitchen, spooned coffee into the percolator and put two slices of bread into the toaster. Then, leaving the machines to do their job, she checked over the one remaining carton that was to go in her car.

It contained pressed flowers, dozens of candles, and all the rest of the paraphernalia needed for her hobby. Confident that she hadn't forgotten anything, she glanced at her watch, and groaned. Zak would be arriving in twenty minutes and she was determined to be ready waiting for him at the wheel of her car.

One thing she couldn't understand was the way he'd capitulated over her wish to drive herself. He'd seemed so adamant about driving her there. But he'd told her he admired an independent spirit, hadn't he? Maybe he'd realised she wouldn't allow him to override her independence.

Annie had given in meekly on one score: she'd agreed to him leading the way to Bowes. Though she had pointed out his car was far more powerful than hers and she'd probably hold him back. However, that hadn't seemed to cause him any concern.

But Annie was concerned when, a quarter of an hour later, she tried in vain to start her car. She'd filled up with petrol the previous afternoon, so it couldn't be that. It was a new car, for heaven's sake; there was no logical reason why it shouldn't start.

Sighing, she flicked the catch to release the bonnet, got out of the car, lifted the bonnet and peered down. She twiddled and pulled at a few things, but couldn't see anything obviously wrong.

'Do you need any help?'

With a sense of déjà vu, Annie looked up. She knew her cheeks were pink; this time, though, bad temper was the cause. She hated not being able to fix something herself.

'It won't start,' she said. 'I don't know why. Will you see if you can spot what's wrong?'

'I would if we had time. But I do want us to get to Bowes before dark.'

'But you're a mechanic. It wouldn't take you long.'

'That would depend on what I found, Annie. I suggest — '

'I wasn't asking for a suggestion. I was asking for help.' Annie crashed the bonnet down. 'Seeing as you won't even look, I'll wait until the garage opens and get someone round. I'll find my own way to Bowes, you needn't hang around wasting precious time.'

Zak shook his head, then reached a long arm into her car. For a moment she thought she'd won, thought he was releasing the bonnet catch. But, no: next thing she knew, he was striding round to the back of the car and opening the hatchback door.

'What do you think you're doing?' She was almost dancing with rage as she joined him.

'Unloading your stuff to put into my car,' he said, lifting out the carton nearest to him. 'It could take all day for someone to locate the fault in yours.'

'So I'll drive up tomorrow.' She tugged desperately at the carton in his arms.

'I think not,' he drawled, her tugging making not the slightest bit of difference to his hold on the carton. 'Tomorrow we have people to meet, and I'm not changing appointments to accommodate your stubbornness.'

'Yesterday you called it independence.' Annie spoke through gritted teeth and gave an extra-hard tug at the carton. He let go of it with a suddenness that surprised her.

The unexpected weight landed against her chest, her body jerked backwards and her ankle gave way. Strong arms shot out to grab her shoulders and, although the carton was a barrier between them, Annie was dizzied into a whirl of sensations as she looked up at him and their glances meshed.

He raised his eyebrows and his square-cut jaw seemed to tighten a fraction, giving her a tantalising glimpse of the small indentation in the centre of his chin which was not quite a dimple.

'One can carry independence too far,' he said mildly. 'You're in my employ, Annie, and I'm going to make sure you're where I want you, when I want you there.'

'Gail and Martyn employ me,' she corrected him.

'No, Annie. The sister company comes entirely under my jurisdiction. And so do you . . . for as long as I want you.'

'I . . . I . . . Oh, all right, I'll come in your blasted car. I know why you're insisting: it's because you think you wouldn't be able to find the fault in my car and then you'd look a fool.' Annie knew she was acting and speaking childishly; nevertheless, she wasn't prepared for his sudden laughter.

'Isn't this rather ridiculous?' he asked, once his laughter had died away. 'Standing here at the crack of dawn, holding this carton and yelling at each other?'

Reluctantly, Annie found her own lips twitching, but she refused to laugh aloud.

'I see you're going prepared for anything.' Zak inclined his head towards the selection of candles in the carton. 'I hope I didn't give you the wrong impression when I said there was no electric blanket. There is electricity laid on.'

'Maybe I just like eating by candlelight,' Annie said. Then wished she hadn't as she had a sudden vision of them sharing a candlelit meal together. 'But, as you say, I'm going prepared for anything.' More visions popped into her head. Cripes, this was going from bad to worse. What was she doing, allowing thoughts like this to creep in?

'So?' she said snappily. 'Are we going to stand here all day? I thought you said you didn't want to waste precious time?'

Annie felt a momentary delight in turning his own words against him. Then wished she hadn't done so, as his expression turned to one of aloofness.

He didn't speak again until they'd transferred all Annie's cases and cartons into the boot of his car. And he'd set a fast pace for doing that, Annie thought resentfully. But she'd forced herself to move as quickly as he had.

'Have you attended to everything in the house?' he asked. 'Turned off the gas, electricity and water? Made sure all the windows are secure?'

'I'd better go and double-check, just

to be sure.' She knew she'd done everything, but Zak had hustled her enough. Now he could wait for a while . . . and serve him right, too.

'It's not like you to be unsure, Annie.' He leant back against his car and folded his arms.

He must have seen through her ruse. He was teasing her. She could tell by his face. And him teasing her did funny things to her insides.

Annie stepped away and hurried into the house. She knew she was unsure of one thing, and that was her feelings for Zak. One second she felt like hitting him, the next . . .

Oh, cripes. What *had* her volunteering let her in for?

6

What have I let myself in for? Annie asked herself the question again as the big, comfortable car silently ate away the miles.

However suitable she was for the job, no way was Zak going to be an easy taskmaster. OK, on occasions a crack appeared and his sunny side broke through, but all too often he showed a darker side. Could she cope with that, or should she try to find a way out?

Oh, how pathetic. Of course she'd be able to cope. She was just apprehensive about going to live and work in a new area where Zak was the only person she knew. She'd got a challenging job; she'd be able to go and visit Geraldine; there'd be new places to explore and new friends to make. And if Zak let Mr Dark, Cold and Aloof take him over, then that was up to him.

No, it isn't entirely up to him, she decided a minute later. It's up to me to try and find the gentle and sympathetic person I know he can be.

Thoughtfully, she sneaked a sideways look at him from beneath her lashes. What she saw on his face drove out all other thoughts. He looked smug and complacent — and a sudden suspicion crept into her mind. He'd had plenty of opportunity the previous evening, hadn't he? Several times he'd been alone in her garage . . . alone with her car. And he was a trained mechanic; it would have been so easy for him . . .

'What did you do?' she asked bluntly.

He made no pretence of not knowing what she was talking about. 'Just removed the engine management chip,' he stated airily. 'Nothing permanent, I assure you.'

Annie wasn't sure if she'd ever heard of one of those before. She wasn't about to admit that to the . . . the rat-fink, though. And in any case, its name made it fairly obvious what it did.

133

'Why?' she asked. 'I can't believe it was for the pleasure of my company.'

'Hardly,' he agreed readily. 'Though I have to admit, you're an attractive travelling companion.' The early morning sun was dancing on her hair through the car windows, highlighting different shades of red. 'You should wear your hair loose more often. It suits you.'

'Don't prevaricate.' The fact he'd paid her a compliment scarcely registered. 'I want to know why you were so determined that I shouldn't use my own car.'

'I thought I'd already made it clear.' He spoke patiently as if explaining something to a child. 'You'll need a four-wheel-drive for the area in which you'll be living. It's bleak moorland up there, Annie. The locals have a saying: 'You'll always remember Bowes Moor in November, when frost and ice abound. Its beauty and hardship and the sound of feet . . . echo the frozen ground'.'

'If that's the case, I can't understand

why you didn't find me somewhere nearer base to live.'

'You're not complaining at the fact you'll have to drive a few miles every day, are you? It's too late to get cold feet now, Annie. You accepted the job and the house that went with it.'

It almost sounded like he was egging her on to complain or argue. Well, tough. She wasn't playing.

Glancing at him, she said sweetly, 'If the locals' quaint saying is to be believed . . . cold feet are to be expected. Perhaps that's why there are two hot-water bottles at the house. One for each foot. I suppose 'the wind blows in the door fit to knock a man off his legs', as well?' she quoted from *Nicholas Nickleby*. Gail had told her that Dotheboys Hall, the academy where the unfortunate pupils had boarded in Charles Dickens' book, had been based on a boys' school in Bowes.

'And I suppose you see me as Wackford Squeers?' Zak drawled in amusement. 'The hard and wicked master who, amongst other things, starved his pupils. Well, I can set your mind at rest on that score. We're approaching the Barnby Moor turn-off. Fancy some breakfast, Annie?'

★　★　★

Zak's warmer side appeared over the meal; he was a Charles Dickens fan and had every book written by or about him.

'My parents started the collection. From me being about nine or ten, a favourite day out was to bookshops or book fairs looking for copies to add to it. You'll have to come and see my library one day,' he told her. 'You obviously enjoy his works, too.'

'Dad used to read Dickens to me for my bedtime stories.' Annie blinked the mistiness from her eyes as she remembered those happy, childhood times. 'Oh, he simplified them, but I used to love repeating all the weird and wonderful names. Pecksniff and Spottletoe were

136

two of my favourites. Katie, my sister, hated those stories; she used to bury her head under her eiderdown and refuse to listen.'

'Vicky used to spend hours curled up with Dickens.' Zak said. 'His books were one of her comforts after we lost our parents. She couldn't read them, of course; just needed to touch them and turn the pages because Mum and Dad had loved them.'

A short silence fell, and then they reached for the tomato ketchup at the same time. Their fingers brushed, their glances met and held; it was a moment of gentle empathy.

Then Zak's eyes hardened and he told her harshly to finish her meal. 'We haven't got all day to sit here. I want to get to Bowes, unload your luggage, and then I want you to drive over to the site so you'll at least have some idea of how long it will take before we can become operational.'

Annie deliberately chewed a couple of mouthfuls very slowly before looking at him again. 'I thought you'd planned on visiting the site tomorrow?'

He pushed his empty plate aside and nodded. 'We'll spend part of tomorrow there as well. I've arranged for us to meet the architect at seven-thirty in the morning. But it will save time if you've already seen what stage everything's at. I also want to be sure you can get yourself there. Call it a practice run if you like.'

'I don't see why I should need a practice run. I think I mentioned once before that I'm perfectly capable of following a map.'

'True, but as you'll find out, there's a bit more to it than that. Now, if you're ready, we'll go. There's still another hour and a half's drive before we get there.'

Annie leaned her elbow on the table, rested her chin in her hand, and watched as he rose fluidly from his chair. 'You know what, Zak?' she said. 'If humans had an engine management chip, I'd pay somebody a good price to show me how to remove yours. Not permanently, of course; just every now and then when you're functioning in overdrive. It would do you good to rest up every now and then.'

Her grey eyes were twinkling with amusement — and how come he hadn't noticed her cute, slightly turned-up nose before? 'You think so?' He couldn't help himself: he stretched across the table and ruffled her hair — then snatched his hand away as if he'd been stung. *What the heck had he done that for?*

Even if she hadn't been the one he considered responsible for jeopardising his sister's marriage — for his sister's crash, for his own nightmare about the crash — he didn't hold with relationships between people who worked together. And playful teasing was often the first step to something more.

That thought was a big mistake, too. *Get out of here, Hunter, while you can walk without embarrassing yourself.* 'I'll pay for the meal and then wait for you in the car, Annie. Try not to be too long.' Then he turned and walked away, his strides long and purposeful.

Outside, Zak was grateful for the fresh breeze and drew in several breaths of cool air. There were a couple of reasons why he was going to find it harder than he'd thought to discomfit Annie. One, the lady didn't rattle easily — OK, she'd got annoyed when he'd refused to look at her car, but her annoyance hadn't lasted long; and when she'd realised he'd immobilised it, she'd seemed more intent on finding out why instead of getting angry.

When he'd mentioned the bleakness of the moor, the cold weather she could expect, then — apart from querying the distance to base — she'd turned the whole thing into a conversation about Charles Dickens. And he, darn it, had enjoyed it.

Being told they were meeting the architect at seven-thirty in the morning hadn't fazed her in the slightest; and when he'd tried to hurry her, she'd turned that against him, too.

As for the second reason ... Zak drew in another long breath. In spite of everything, he enjoyed being with her. He appreciated her sense of humour. He liked the way she didn't fly into a temper, the way she didn't sulk. Oh, he'd no doubt she'd fight her own corner, if and when it came to it. She was no 'yes-woman'. Most of all, he fancied her.

But this had to stop. She'd caused both Vicky and him heartache, and he couldn't allow her to get away with that.

He unlocked his car and got in. When Annie joined him he'd keep his mind solely on work ... and the difficulties he'd make sure she would have to face in the coming weeks — starting later today.

7

Once they were on their way, Zak asked for — and listened to — Annie's opinions on the staff they'd need, then told her that he hoped they'd be going to look over a couple of planes in the very near future.

'Both sound suitable; I expect it will come down to which one's the better value for money. I've almost decided on a Chief Engineer — we'll be meeting him soon, he's coming down from Edinburgh.' He flicked a glance at her. 'I'll be interested in your opinion of him.'

'I don't know anything about the technical side of things,' she said in some alarm. 'I can't tell you who'd be suitable for — '

'I want you to weigh up his personality, that's all, Annie. His qualifications are excellent.'

'Is he married?' Annie asked. To her mind it was an important question: if he were married, they'd need to be sure that his wife would be perfectly willing to move. An unwilling partner could have a bad effect on a person's work.

'You'd prefer a married man, would you?'

His tone hadn't changed. It was the ambiguity of the question that stung her.

In a cold, hard voice, staring determinedly ahead, she told Zak the reason for her question. Then she took refuge in silence. She certainly wasn't going to say any more.

Zak didn't speak again either. They'd taken the Scotch Corner turn-off, and Annie knew it wouldn't be too long before they reached their destination. And it couldn't be soon enough for her. She needed space from this man who, as usual, was causing her too many conflicting emotions.

Staring through the window, she started to play the alphabet game with vehicles' registration plates. The old childhood game might calm her.

She was looking for a number plate with the letter D in it when the car slowed and Zak pointed out a building set back slightly from the road.

'A barn?' Annie shrugged. She didn't know or care why he'd drawn her attention to it. But . . .

'That's where you keep your vehicle,' he informed her tersely.

'I thought you said you'd found me a garage in the village?' Annie took in her surroundings at last; she wouldn't have called this area a village.

'It is almost in the village; the main part is about half-a-mile ahead. If you remember, Gail mentioned your house was on the outskirts.'

He made a right turn on to what looked little more than a track. A steep and narrow track winding upwards, which seemed to peter out into a bridleway ahead. Just before that point, however, they curved to the left — and there it was.

Surrounded by a stone wall with iron gates set into it was a grim, gaunt, grey building facing a hill. It had all the bleakness and mystery of the moors about it. One lone tree in the garden stood sentinel — its almost bare branches, close to the upstairs window, would undoubtedly tap and creak against the glass on a windy night. With its tall chimneys, one of which had a cowl, it was like something out of a Gothic novel.

Annie fell in love with it immediately. Discovering this was to be her home for the next few months cast away any thoughts she might have had of trying to find a way out of her situation.

She almost leapt out of the car and hurried to the gates. 'High Moor House,' she said aloud, her fingers tracing the words formed in wrought iron on the left-hand gate.

'I told you it was isolated.' Zak had joined her and, turning to look at him, she got the impression he was tensely waiting for her reaction. *Bless*. How she'd misjudged him earlier; she'd thought he was egging her on to complain, but all the time he'd had this surprise in store for her. True, there was still the inside to see, but she just *knew* she'd love that too.

Full of pleasure, she went up on her tiptoes, put her arms on his shoulders and kissed his cheek. And the tingle that ran through her veins when she stepped back was just excitement over her living accommodation, wasn't it?

'It's perfect, Zak. The sort of house I've always dreamed of living in. How did you know? Did Gail tell you?'

Zak cursed inwardly. She wasn't meant to *like* the place. 'You won't feel frightened being here alone?' he asked. 'It's an old house. The villagers probably think it's haunted.'

Annie laughed throatily. 'I'll be disappointed if there isn't a ghost or two,' she told him. 'Let's get my luggage inside, Zak. We'll just dump it in the hall and then we can get straight off to the site. The sooner we get there, the sooner I can get back here and explore. Have you got the door key, or is it under a stone or something?'

Zak reached into his pocket and, without speaking, handed her a key ring with two keys on.

It took Annie all her effort not to run up the crazy-paving path that led to the front door. And once she'd opened the door, it was even more of an effort not to go all the way in and soak up the atmosphere.

One excited glance at the square hall with its black-and-white tiled floor — partly covered by a deep red Afghan design rug — the old-fashioned doors leading into rooms off the hall, and the wide staircase with a wooden banister, was enough for her to know she'd been right. She was going to love the inside of the house, too.

But, leaving the door open wide, she retraced her way back down the path, out of the iron gates and over to the car. Zak was still standing where she'd left him, an unreadable expression on his face; though if she had to hazard a guess, she'd say he was slightly stunned. Maybe he hadn't expected her to like the house?

'Could you unlock the boot?' she prompted. 'The sooner we're unloaded, the sooner we can go.'

★　★　★

There was still that tenseness about him as he drove them back down the track; a nerve seemed to be twitching just above his tight jawline. Even his voice contained a tone she hadn't heard before when, after drawing up in front of the barn, he reached for another set of keys. 'Padlock key and ignition key.' He held them out to her.

'Thanks. I'll follow you, shall I?' she said as she got out.

This time, when she'd unlocked the padlock and opened the door, she didn't like what she saw at all.

Inside the barn, as though mocking her, was an ex-Army Jeep. She'd seen enough of them in films and on television to guess they hadn't been designed with comfort in mind.

Now Zak's comments about a practice run made sense. That was so not funny. It would take more than one journey before she felt confident with this left-hand-drive monster.

'It's the same model as I'll be using.' Again, he'd come up behind her. 'They're cold and uncomfortable, the very devil to handle until you get used to them, but totally suitable for the area.'

Was he trying to worry her with his talk of the house being haunted and the Jeep being a devil to handle?

'I've never driven one but I've always wanted to.' *Put that in your fuel tank and see how far you'll get.* Annie even managed to produce something like a smile for him to follow her outrageous lie.

He looked slightly disconcerted, and she gave a genuine smile as she handed back the keys. 'Perhaps, just for this first time, it would be better if you backed it out for me.'

★ ★ ★

When they arrived at the airfield an hour later, every bone and muscle in Annie's body was aching. After bringing the vehicle to a halt, she slowly clambered down from it, watched by Zak. She stretched and groaned in protest along with her body.

'You didn't manage too badly, I thought,' he stated unsmilingly. 'It would cost us extra time, but I suppose we could look around for something easier for you to handle.'

'No way. This is fine,' Annie returned, in a fit of stubborn pride. 'Monster and I will soon get used to each other.' *I'll soon get used to having my bones rattled, my muscles stretched and twisted.*

'Monster?' Zak frowned down at her.

'Mmm. What other name could one give to such a vehicle?' she said, patting the bonnet.

She turned to look at the building; it was slightly larger than Edmunds' but in other respects almost a replica . . . on the outside at least. 'It's going to be home from home,' she told him. 'Come on, let's go inside. There must be at least three people to see.' Annie pointed to a couple of cars — both with four-wheel-drive, she noted — and a van which was parked near them.

'The van is the builder's; one car belongs to Fiona, my secretary, and the other to her parents, though I don't know what they're doing here. The plumber is conspicuous by his absence, as are the heating contractors.' Zak frowned. 'I had hoped the central heating was being installed today. Still,' he added, 'we've got cloakroom and kitchen facilities. They were the first priority. Until they were finished, we had to run across to the Portakabin.'

Has Zak guessed what I need right now? Annie wondered, as they walked towards the building. Loo, followed by a cup of coffee. 'In this instance your priorities are spot on,' she said mischievously.

She realised she was enjoying herself. Though she knew before long she'd want to try and analyse Zak's attitude, and work out if the lonely situation of the house and the Monster had been his way of testing her reactions. Then her enjoyment would be replaced by . . . By what? she asked herself.

But there was no time to ponder that question, for the door was flung open just as they reached it and Annie watched as a girl, who looked a few years younger than her, threw herself eagerly into Zak's arms.

'Zak,' she said breathlessly, 'I've missed you so much, I'm so glad you're back.'

'It's good to be back, Fee.' Zak held the girl slightly away from him and smiled down into her face. As Annie looked on, something twisted inside her. Twisted and hurt.

Oh, heavens. Cupid had turned traitor and disregarded her pleas. She was jealous. And that meant . . .

That meant, against all the odds . . . she'd fallen in love. She knew the colour was draining from her face as realisation hit, and at the same moment Zak turned to introduce the two girls.

'Annie, I'd like you to meet my temporary secretary, Fiona Dunne.'

After a cursory greeting, Fiona turned back to Zak. 'Soon to be permanent, I hope. You promised you'd think about it, Zak.' She pouted prettily and again Zak smiled down into her face.

'A good secretary should always offer coffee,' he admonished teasingly. 'Annie . . . ' He turned his gaze to her with no sign of a smile. ' . . . Annie looks as though she needs one.'

'Oh, Mum's seeing to the coffee, she's brought some of your favourite biscuits, too. Dad's here as well.' Fiona took a possessive hold on Zak's arm and led him through the door.

Leaving me to follow like a tame dog, Annie thought sourly, jealousy gnawing away at her. The cloakrooms were conveniently next to the main door, and after throwing a despairing look at Zak and Fiona, so absorbed in each other, Annie slipped into the Ladies.

After washing her hands, she stared in dismay at her reflection in the mirror: a white face and huge grey eyes stared back at her. 'How could I have fallen in love with him?' she muttered angrily. She didn't do relationships any more. Especially with someone who wasn't to be trusted. And Zak was one of those.

He'd let her think he was from the Air Ministry, he'd changed the terms of her contract by bringing the date forward, and he'd given her that awful vehicle to drive. What's more, when he'd found out about her relationship with a married man — a man she hadn't known was married — he'd judged her without even asking for her side of the story.

He had her down as a marriage-breaker, and he'd made it clear how he felt on that score. She could just imagine how he'd react if he had any idea of her feelings for him.

That brought her to her senses. There was no way she could allow him to guess how she felt. Swiftly, she delved into her handbag to find some make-up; she never wore much, often didn't bother with any at all, but now she felt the need of some.

Hurriedly, she brushed her hair; and, suddenly recalling that Zak had told her she should wear it loose more often, perversely screwed it into a topknot and secured it with a couple of clips she found at the bottom of her bag. Then she took a few deep breaths and went to find Zak and Fiona.

'Ah, here you are, Annie.' Zak detached himself from the small group clustered round what would undoubtedly be the reception desk, then, with a light hand on her elbow, drew her into the group to make the introductions.

Uncomfortably aware of Fiona's resentful gaze, Annie smiled and chatted brightly to the builders, then gratefully accepted a cup of coffee from Mr Dunne and a delicious-looking biscuit from his wife.

She'd felt an immediate rapport with Fiona's parents, who insisted upon Annie calling them Bill and Jackie. 'After all,' said Jackie with a smile, 'we are going to be quite close neighbours. Our farm is in Cotherstone, about five miles from High Moor House.'

Jackie glanced around then spoke in a low voice. 'I do hope you'll be all right there on your own. I can't understand why Zak didn't stick to his original plan. When he first asked if he could rent the two houses, I was under the impression that he'd live in High Moor and you'd be having the smaller one nearer the village.'

'High Moor House is no place for a girl on her own,' Bill agreed gruffly. 'I think I'll have a few words to say to Zak.'

'No, please don't,' Annie beseeched quietly. 'Actually, I love what little I've seen of the house.' Even though Zak obviously did have reasons of his own for deciding she should live there.

'And I'm not just saying it because you own it,' she added, seeing the disbelief on both their faces. 'I'm longing to get away and explore the inside,' she continued. 'I've only seen the hall so far. Zak was anxious for me to try my skills out on the Jeep.'

'You've not driven that thing all the way here?' Jackie said indignantly. 'That's no easy journey for the first time. Or have you driven one before?'

'No, she hadn't.' Zak spoke smoothly from behind them. 'She didn't do too badly as it happens, though I did offer to get her something else. An offer she refused. She's tougher than she looks, aren't you, Annie?'

'I must admit, I thought how frail and pale you looked, Annie.' Fiona had shadowed Zak, and was smiling sweetly with her mouth while her eyes sparked dislike.

'It's been a long day.' Annie spoke calmly. 'You're not seeing me at my best. I'll try and make up for that tomorrow, I'll be fine after a night's sleep.'

'At least you won't have to cook for yourself this evening,' said Jackie. 'That's why we popped in on our way back from market. To invite you and Zak for a meal. We'll drop you off at High Moor, Annie; Zak can pick you up later and bring you to our place.'

'No.' Annie shook her head. 'I mean, thank you, I'd love to come for a meal, but I'll find my own way there.'

She couldn't bring herself to turn down the well-meant invitation, but going out for a meal was the last thing Annie wanted. She needed to be alone to come to think things over. Discovering that she had fallen in love with Zak appalled her. She had to work out some way of defending herself.

'How?' Jackie interrupted her tormented thoughts. 'How will you find your own way? You won't have the Jeep. You're leaving that here, Annie, we're taking you back. I insist.'

'I'll need the Jeep to get me here in

the morning,' Annie explained. 'We're meeting the architect.'

'That's right,' Zak agreed. 'I've fixed a seven-thirty appointment.'

'No problem there. It's my delivery day tomorrow.' Jackie turned to Annie. 'We make traditional farmhouse Cotherstone cheese, Annie,' she explained. 'I've got to have some in Darlington for eight o'clock. I'll fetch you and drop you off here.'

'Seeing as you've got it all planned out, Jackie, you'd better hang on for half an hour while I show Annie what stage everything's at,' said Zak; and, taking her arm, he led her away.

'You've certainly twisted Bill and Jackie around your little finger,' he said coldly, the minute they were out of hearing distance.

'That's more than I can say for your Fiona,' retorted Annie, jealousy making her bitter.

'You don't like her?' Zak's eyes narrowed as he asked the question.

'I didn't say that. I think it's more

that she doesn't like me.' Annie gave a tight smile and changed the subject. 'I can't see that there's much more work to be done here.'

'No, with any luck a couple of weeks should be enough. What we need to decide on is the best place for the office and a storeroom. Once they're done, it'll be down to prettying up, decorating and carpeting.'

Annie found it hard to concentrate, and just hoped and prayed she was making the right sort of comments.

'OK, that will do for now. You look worn out, Annie. As you said, it's been a long day.'

Was she imagining it, or had he spoken with gentleness and concern? Wishful thinking, she told herself; but again she caught a strange expression on his face, a sort of bewilderment, though quickly masked.

'And, as *you* said, Zak, I'm tougher than I look,' she said quietly. I hope that's true, she added silently. I'm going to need to be tough.

* * *

As though sensing her need to be quiet, neither Bill nor Jackie spoke much at first on the homebound journey. But after a while, Jackie began to tell Annie a little about High Moor House.

'There's an oil-fired Aga in the kitchen, we set it going again about a month ago, so everywhere will be well-aired and warm. It supplies your hot water and a few radiators. But it can be a draughty old place, Annie, especially in winter.

'It's reasonably well-furnished, we moved some of the better pieces back in after the summer lettings had ended. And we re-carpeted everywhere about a year ago. I should use the small bedroom at the front, there's a good comfortable bed in there.'

'Is that the one where the tree peeps in the window?'

'We'll lop a few branches off if the noise frightens you,' said Bill. 'I still don't think it's right . . . you being there on your own.'

'I like the sound of branches against glass,' Annie assured him. 'Honestly, I'm going to enjoy living there.' As much as I can enjoy anything when I've done the most stupid thing in my life and fallen in love with Zak Hunter, she acknowledged silently.

Two hours later, Annie firmly decided that even being in love with Zak would not spoil the pleasure that the house gave her. True, she wouldn't like to live here for ever; there was something slightly lacking, though she couldn't put a name to what it was.

It's something to do with the inside, she mused. The outside of the house and the setting is perfect. 'Unrequited love is making you fanciful,' she jeered at herself. 'Well, that's better than falling to pieces,' she argued. 'And that's what will happen if you don't watch yourself. You're on the road to heartache if you let your feelings show. Just remember that.'

It was hard to stop those feelings

from showing when she opened the door to Zak. Wearing a dazzling white loose-knit sweater, which threw his gleaming black hair into prominence, and slim-fitting, exquisitely-cut black trousers, he was a heart-stopper on legs again — with bells on. Warmth crept over every inch of Annie's body, turning her insides to marshmallow.

'You look fully recovered, Annie. In fact you look delightful . . . like the Spirit of Autumn. Your hair's the same colour as the leaves that are tumbling from the trees and covering my garden.'

She'd changed into a soft swirling dress, with a low-waisted, finely-pleated skirt, in gold and coppery shades; and she knew her newly-washed hair would be gleaming as the glow from the overhead light played on it.

Time stood still as Annie, one hand on the open front door, looked up at him. Slowly, his dark head descended, blocking out the moonlight from behind him. She felt the warmth of his mouth on hers . . . the little ghost kisses whispering against her flesh, the slight roughness of his cheek.

She felt herself kissing him back. Breathing in the cool but exciting tang of his aftershave, she was aware of every muscle and sinew in his body.

At the same time she had the sensation of drowning, felt weak and tingly, and her heartbeat echoed frantically in her ears as she made a small whimpering noise in her throat.

Then his lips stilled, his body tensed. Now she could feel his anger as his fingers cruelly gripped her shoulders . . . not pulling her close . . . levering her away. She had to do something, had to think of something to say, had to speak before he did; anything he said would be hurtful and would shrivel her up into a sick knot of hopelessness.

'Did Fiona turn you down?' She hadn't realised she was capable of injecting such sneering ice into her voice, and although her heart was breaking she couldn't help feeling proud of herself when she noted his

164

tight-lipped look.

But she shrivelled anyway as he stared hard at her, and his tone was vitriolic when he grated, 'At least Fiona doesn't break up marriages and wreck other people's lives. She didn't ask about the marital status of prospective employees.'

'Perhaps that's because she isn't experienced in — '

'You don't have to remind me of how experienced *you* are, Annie. Unfortunately, I'm all too well aware of that fact.'

'I thought that's why I was asked to volunteer for the job, because of my experience?'

'Oh, yes, your various experiences were the main reasons. I'll tell you something, though, I didn't realise you'd had acting experience. You really managed to fool Bill and Jackie: they phoned me to congratulate me on my choice. They think you're sweet and gentle and kind. Oh yes, you fooled them all right.'

'Well, I'd hate to disillusion them by being any later than we already are. Tardiness is the height of bad manners.'

'As I told you once before . . . you're one heck of a lady, Annie.' This time his words had a completely different meaning, and Annie knew it. She also had a feeling that any antagonism he'd shown towards her so far was merely a pale foretaste of things to come.

8

'Ugh. How I hate early November mornings,' Jackie said as Annie, well wrapped against the bitter cold, settled herself in the passenger seat. 'Did you sleep well? Was the bed comfortable? There was a really hard frost last night. Were you warm enough?'

'Well, I didn't want to get up, that's for sure.' Annie gave a rueful smile. 'Two dark o'clocks on a trot are a bit much to take.'

'You mustn't let Zak overwork you,' Jackie stated, after negotiating an awkward bend. 'He's always tended to work long hours, but he isn't usually so thoughtless towards his colleagues.'

'I guess he's just eager to get everything up and running quickly,' said Annie.

'Maybe.' Jackie shrugged. 'But he's changed recently. It's like he's angry with himself and, at times, he takes his anger out on others.'

'When you say recently, do you mean since his sister's accident?'

'Yes, I suppose I do. I think he blames himself for it. You see, usually if Vicky needed him, he'd drive down to see her. But on the day of the accident he had an important meeting and couldn't get away. So Vicky decided to come and see him.'

'It's strange how people tend to blame themselves when something like that happens,' said Annie.

'Tell me about it.' Jackie sighed. 'I feel guilty about what happened to Vicky, too. No, not the accident, though that's part of the whole sorry mess. Vicky always used to spend a lot of time with us. She and Fiona grew up together.

'Vicky met her husband at our house. His parents, John and Vanessa Blane, are two of our greatest friends. Actually, they live in Suffolk, do you know them?'

'No. But Fiona pointed them out to me on the photos she showed me last night while you were in the kitchen making that gorgeous dessert.'

Annie frowned as she recalled Zak's attitude when she'd been looking at one particular photo: a party scene with himself standing close to Fiona, the Blanes with a man wearing a party hat, and Jackie holding a huge cake with candles on . . .

'Who do you recognise, Annie?' Zak had asked.

'You, Fiona and Jackie,' she'd replied, puzzled at Zak's tone.

'Look closer,' he'd insisted.

'Oh, the man with a silly hat. He uses Edmunds' quite regularly.'

'So you do know him then?' Zak had asked, staring intently at her.

'He flies to London once every two or three weeks. Or he used to. And I think he was on the Amsterdam flight a couple of times. He wasn't one of 'my' regulars, though, which is why I didn't recognise him at first. I haven't seen him at all since I went back after my time off. But why the interrogation, Zak? Has he made a complaint against Edmunds'?'

Jackie had called to them to come and sit down at that point, so Annie's question had gone unanswered . . .

Shrugging away the memory of the strange conversation, Annie turned to Jackie. 'So that party was the first time Vicky met the man who became her husband?'

'It was a whirlwind romance: they'd only known each other six months before they married. And from what I can work out, it's a case of 'Marry in haste, repent at leisure'. Vicky didn't seem to adapt at all; she was left on her own a lot in an alien area. She's got John and Vanessa close by, but that's not the same, is it?'

'She'd probably find it hard to tell her in-laws she's unhappy,' said Annie.

'Zak was worried about Vicky from the word go,' Jackie continued. 'They were always close, he was father and big brother rolled into one. Probably a bit over-protective and he certainly gave her almost anything she wanted. She didn't act spoilt, though. In fact, you remind me of her in a way. You've got the same serenity Vicky had before her marriage.'

Is that another reason for Zak blowing hot and cold? wondered Annie. I don't stand a chance. Not only do I remind him of the hurt he caused his wife, I remind him of how his sister used to be, too. He did say something about it once.

'When did Zak's marriage break up?' she asked aloud.

'He's never been married. He nearly was, a couple of years ago. But Helen couldn't take to Vicky. I think she was jealous of Zak's protectiveness towards his sister. Helen wanted all of him, all his attention for herself.

'Fiona was glad when it broke up; she's always worshipped Zak, though I keep telling her she's too young for him. Still, who knows? Zak will have to settle down one day.'

So, I was wrong, thought Annie. Zak isn't taking any of his own guilt out on me. He wasn't unfaithful to his wife; he's never been married. But why should he taunt me so much just because I unwittingly had a relationship with a married man? He didn't act the way he does towards me until he found that out. Oh, what a mess.

The irony of it was, she realised now, that what she'd felt before hadn't been love at all. She'd thought it was at the time; so much so she'd sworn off ever falling in love again. But she hadn't met Zak then.

'Look, Annie, I'm very fond of Zak. I can't understand why he seems to be treating you so badly. The house and the Jeep, crack of dawn appointments . . . it isn't like him to be so inconsiderate. I know we've only just met, but . . . well, if you need someone to talk to . . . '

'You know, don't you?' whispered Annie. 'You've guessed how I feel about him. I couldn't have let it show. I couldn't.' *Huh! What about the way you kissed him back last night?* But, no. Surely she'd covered that up all right by challenging him?

'No, I don't think you let it show. I can't say how I guessed, really. Feminine intuition, I suppose.'

'Don't you mind? I mean, well, I know nothing will come of it, but you said Fiona — '

'Yes, I said Fiona had always worshipped him. And in a way, I'd like Zak for a son-in-law. But, deep down, I know our Fee isn't the right one for him. Anyway, I just thought I'd mention everything, and . . . '

'Thank you, Jackie. I appreciate it, and I might need someone to talk to, one day. But I've got to try and sort things out for myself first.'

'That's settled then.' Jackie nodded and went on to talk of other things, giving Annie a chance to try and pull herself together.

★ ★ ★

When they arrived at the site, Annie was relieved to see the building was in darkness.

'We're early,' said Jackie. 'Do you want me to wait until Zak or the architect arrives?'

Annie shook her head. 'Zak gave me my own keys yesterday. I'm not familiar with the whereabouts of the light switches yet, but I brought a torch with me. You get off, Jackie, I'll be fine.'

With any luck, she thought, as she watched Jackie drive away, there'd be time for a coffee before Zak or the architect got here — time to ponder over why Zak was Mr Nice Guy one minute and Mr Not Nice the next.

On second thoughts, she decided as she unlocked the door, her time would be better spent thinking about work.

On third thoughts . . . She gasped as she stepped into an indoor rainstorm! She'd better find out pretty darned quick what had activated the fire-sprinklers.

174

No smoke, no fire, no heat . . . safe to leave the door open and let the water stream out. Not safe to turn on the lights.

Thank heavens she'd brought her torch; the utility room which housed the stop valve — she hoped — was right at the far end of the building. Good job she was wearing boots; the water was a good few centimetres deep.

There. She'd made it. She flashed her torch around, spotted the stop valve, but . . . *Where was the key for the padlock on the strap around the valve?* She couldn't de-activate the sprinklers until she'd got the strap off.

*   *   *

Driving to the site, Zak marvelled at the way Lady Luck had dealt an extra card into his hand, and congratulated himself on being able to play it in his private vendetta against Annie without being cast as the 'bad boy'.

When he'd arrived home last night

after dropping Annie off, there'd been a message from the architect on his answerphone, changing the seven-thirty meeting to nine o'clock. All grist to the mill when it came to making Annie's life hard.

After all, he could say quite truthfully that he'd thought it had been too late to phone her. Had thought she'd already be in bed asleep. And he'd been thinking of Jackie, too. He hadn't wanted to get her out of bed to tell her not to pick Annie up.

He wondered if Annie would kick up a fuss when she realised she could have had an extra hour and a half in bed. He hoped so. Nothing he'd done so far had caused the reaction he'd expected. She loved the house in the middle of nowhere, and had given the Jeep a pet name.

What about last night when he'd kissed her?

He'd *known* she'd kiss him back.

That was different. A mistake. Sure, there was a strong attraction between them. And that was putting it mildly. But that definitely wasn't part of his plan. Kissing Annie — wanting to know Annie much better — was off-limits.

But he could still remember the way she'd responded; could still taste her lips, still smell her perfume.

Determinedly, he conjured up another picture. Vicky with bruises on her face and the jagged cut that was likely to leave a scar. That accident had happened because Vicky was upset by the knowledge her husband had been seeing someone.

And, it was obvious now that it was Annie he'd been seeing. He thought again what a good actress she was. She'd made it seem as though she hardly recognised his brother-in-law when she'd seen him on that photo last night.

That was better. If he had to feel anything for Annie Layton, then best it be anger. Anger and loathing. But he mustn't let her see that. They had to work together and he wanted the expansion to be a success. He'd have to be

177

careful not to overplay his hand, not to cause her so much hardship that she'd quit.

Almost there . . . He turned left onto the tarmacadam driveway that led to the airfield-to-be, and gave a half-smile as he saw the lights shining out from the building a distance ahead. He'd soon see Annie's reaction to the news the architect wouldn't be joining them until nine o'clock.

As he got closer, the half-smile froze. The lights he'd seen were coming from the Portakabin. The main building wasn't so brightly lit; it looked as if the storm lanterns were in use.

He increased his speed, then came to a jerky halt, leaped out of his vehicle and cursed profusely. There was water streaming out through the open door.

He dashed inside and saw Annie looking remarkably like the way she had the first time he'd met her — with soaking wet corkscrew curls and water trickling down her face. She was talking on the telephone. She replaced the handset just as he reached her side.

'What the heck's happened, Annie?' he demanded.

'Seeing as nobody was here when I arrived, I decided to take a shower. Shame you arrived too late to join me.'

Zak stared at her. *Didn't anything rattle this woman's cage?*

'Luckily, I managed to find the key for the stop valve and I turned the sprinklers off,' she said.

'Sprinklers?' Zak looked up and was rewarded with a few drops of water plopping into his eyes. 'There wasn't a fire, was there? I can't smell smoke. Annie, are you all right? You're not hurt?' He grabbed her shoulders, drew her close and stared down into her face.

'Not hurt. Just wet.' *And just wanting to stay here in your arms.*

'But what happened?' he asked again. His breath was warm on her cold, wet face. She stepped back out of his arms. 'I didn't have any of the contractors' phone numbers,' she said, 'so I phoned the fire station. The fire officer I spoke to reckons the frost must have caused a water pipe in the sprinklers' system to burst, and that set the heads going.'

Zak picked up one of the lanterns and began to wander round, feeling the walls.

'I think the floor and I got the worst of it,' said Annie. 'It was just so lucky we had to be here early. Another half hour or so and there'd have been a proper flood to deal with. As it is, we'll have to wait for everywhere to dry out, and then get an electrician in to do a safety check before the builders and decorators can carry on with their work.'

She shivered suddenly and wrapped her arms around herself.

Zak shrugged out of his jacket, pulled his sweater off and handed it to her. 'Go over to the Portakabin and get your wet things off, Annie. There are some towels there, and there should be a boiler suit or some overalls. You can put my sweater on underneath. It won't be catwalk fashion, but at least you'll be warm and dry.'

Holding it away from her wet sheepskin, Annie clasped the sweater tightly. It was still warm from Zak's body, and she knew it would smell of Zak; she fought against the urge to bury her face in it. Besides, she'd have found it hard to tear her gaze away from the black vee at the open-neck of Zak's shirt and the very masculine chest beneath the shirt, the broad shoulders . . . *This was ridiculous.* She cleared her throat in an effort to ease her dry mouth.

Zak blinked to clear his mind of unwanted thoughts, and prayed Annie hadn't guessed them. He couldn't meet her eyes; he looked down at her wet boots.

'We might be able to do something about footwear when Fee arrives,' he said. 'She usually wears boots for driving and brings shoes to change into. Says her feet get too hot if she wears boots all day, but I think she wears high heels because they make her legs look good.' *There.* If Annie had guessed his thoughts, that last remark might make her think she'd guessed wrong.

OK, so his darling Fee will look good, and I'll look like a badly-wrapped bundle from somebody's dustbin. Somehow, though, Annie managed a smile.

'It'll be good to feel warm again,' she said. 'Perhaps you could phone the electrician while I'm changing, and then, you might make me a coffee? It'll have to be instant, of course, we can't use the percolator. It's a good job the cooker runs on Calor gas.'

'I had worked that one out,' Zak replied tersely.

'You sound like you need a coffee, too. Oh, if you've got the architect's mobile number, you'd better phone him as well. He's obviously been held up somewhere, but you might be able to put him off,' she added as she made her way towards the door.

Things might have backfired this morning. And how, Zak thought. But he could turn it to his advantage. Annie was probably looking forward to having the weekend off. 'I'll see if I can reschedule it for Saturday.'

'Good idea,' Annie said over her shoulder. 'Today and tomorrow should be long enough to dry things out in here, but we don't want to waste another two days just because it's the weekend.'

She stopped at the door and turned round. 'Not that today and Friday will be wasted. I'll set up office in the Portakabin and, amongst other things, draft out adverts for the local newspaper and appropriate magazines.'

'Fine,' said Zak. 'Let me check them over before you place them.'

'Of course.' Annie replied calmly, but inside she was wondering if Zak would want to check over everything she did . . . or, worse — would he be looking to find fault?

9

During the next few days, it became clear to Annie that one of her worries at least was unfounded. Zak was treating her with a cool respect in all matters relating to the business. Even to the point of almost apologising after their first meeting with the prospective Chief Engineer.

Towards the end of that meeting, Zak had glanced at her, a question in his eyes, and she'd nodded. She liked what she'd seen of the interviewee.

And when it seemed fairly obvious Zak was about to offer him the position, Anthony had said: 'If I were to be offered the post, I'd like to bring my wife to meet you, and to show her around the place before making a decision.

'You see — ' He'd turned to Annie at this point, and smiled. ' — she wants to be sure that I'll be happy in my working environment. She says she'll follow me to the ends of the earth as long as she knows it's the right place for me. It's so important for both partners in a marriage to be sure about things like this.'

Zak had responded: 'I know I'm speaking for both of us when I say that those sentiments are admirable. In fact, we'd like your wife to come and meet us as soon as possible. And, yes, that does mean we'd like you to join us as Chief Engineer.'

Later, Zak said, 'I have to admit, you do know what you're talking about, Annie. You've got a knack of knowing what will matter to people.'

* * *

Those compliments kept her walking on air for a while. True, the knowledge of her love for him still hurt her, and jealousy still gnawed at her when she saw him and Fiona together. And Fiona seemed to make plenty of opportunities to 'need a word with' Zak.

According to Fiona, she and Zak were spending most evenings together after work, too. Annie fought to keep her morale up by constantly telling herself that Zak didn't seem to have anything other than a friendly attitude towards Fiona.

However, it was Annie and not Zak to whom Fiona appealed one particular morning. Annie was in the newly-completed office — not exactly *completed*, for it still needed carpeting. But it was private, and did contain a desk, three chairs, a telephone and a cafetière.

And it was somewhere for Annie to interview the prospective employees who'd be her responsibility, though she wasn't expecting to do that for a couple of days yet. They'd only just placed those vacancies with the local Job Centre.

She had met and liked Zak's friend, Edward Grayson, who would captain one of the two crews; and, as Zak himself was intending to captain a crew, that was the pilots sorted out for the time being.

They'd already held interviews for an Assistant Engineer and two ground engineers. Anthony, who'd accepted the post after bringing his wife to meet them, had been there to have his say in the choice of engineering staff.

Yes, everything was running smoothly, and she was managing to cope with her feelings reasonably well. Annie was silently praising herself when Fiona burst into the office.

'Annie, somebody's here. I think she's come for an interview, but I'm not sure which job she's interested in.'

'Didn't you ask her?' Annie queried in surprise.

'I couldn't. She . . . Oh, Annie, I know it sounds awful, but I don't know how to . . . I feel embarrassed . . . I don't know how to cope with her. She showed me a card. She's deaf and can't speak, but she can read and write. That's what the card says. Oh, and her name is Jill.'

'Go back to her and tell her I'll see her,' said Annie. 'Then bring her in.'

'But . . . but, she won't be able to hear me.'

'Look at her while you're speaking, talk normally, don't shout. She'll probably lip-read your words. Ask her to follow you, and if she doesn't respond, take her arm gently and bring her in.'

Annie's calm manner rubbed off on the younger girl and, nodding, Fiona hurried out.

'Do you want me to stay?' Fiona asked on returning with Jill.

'No, it's all right, Fiona. We'll manage.' And Annie smiled at Jill, who flashed her card again, then produced another.

This second card, presumably written by Jill for the occasion, had a brief sentence: 'I can also cook.'

Not only that, she's got a sense of humour, acknowledged Annie, her lips quirking as she pointed to a chair. She'd obviously come about the caterer's position.

Jill visibly relaxed and, producing a

notepad and pen, pushed them across the desk to Annie. However, Annie shook her head. She knew a bit of sign language and the Finger Alphabet. She'd learned them when a deaf passenger had travelled regularly on the London flight.

So, using her hands and fingers, she spoke to Jill in a mixture of both — resorting to spelling out a complete word when she couldn't sign the shorter version.

Jill clapped her own hands in delighted surprise before signing a reply to Annie.

The interview continued smoothly until, after one of Annie's signed questions, Jill chuckled and shook her head. She reached for the pad and drew a couple of diagrams.

Annie giggled: she'd mistakenly asked the question, 'Have you had any experience in preparing bullets?' The fingers used to portray 'f' and 'l' were quite similar; Annie, of course, had meant to sign 'buffets'.

'Gosh. What an idiot,' Annie said in self-disgust, and at that precise second the door opened and Zak entered. She was aware of her eyes widening in horror as she saw the look on his face. She'd never seen such naked anger there before, and wondered frantically what could be wrong . . .

⋆　⋆　⋆

Before he'd walked into the office, Zak had been feeling as if a huge weight had been lifted from him. Vicky's phone call had done that. She'd told him about a letter Oliver had shown her from the woman he'd been seeing:

'He showed it me to prove it was all over between him and Lindy.'

'Lindy?' Zak queried, scared to hope. 'Did you say 'Lindy'?'

'Yes. That's what she's called, the one Oliver had been seeing. She said she was glad they'd ended things, and hoped he could mend his marriage. And I think we'll be able to, Zak. I really do.'

'I'm glad, Vicky,' Zak told her. And after a while, hoping he'd said the right things in the right places, he was relieved when the conversation ended.

He knew now Annie hadn't been acting when she'd seen the photo of his brother-in-law and denied knowing him. And, deep down, he'd always thought Annie had told the truth when she'd said she'd had no idea that the man she was seeing was married — and she'd finished it the second she discovered he was.

If that man *had* been his brother-in-law, then a business relationship with Annie was the only thing Zak could have allowed himself. Now, though, knowing Annie was truthful — which his heart had believed all along — he could now admit to himself that he loved her.

True, there was a mountain to climb first; he'd have to explain everything to her, and hope she might be able to forgive him for the way he'd treated her.

Just before the phone call from Vicky,

Fee had told him Annie was interviewing. She might have finished by now, and he'd see if she'd agree to him taking her for a meal this evening. If she did, he'd tell her everything.

There was a good chance she'd understand. Annie had such a caring attitude towards others — especially when they were vulnerable, he told himself, as he opened the door to Annie's office.

And saw and heard the way she was behaving towards the interviewee . . .

★   ★   ★

'I think I'd better take this interview over,' he grated harshly, closing the door and leaning against it.

'All right,' agreed Annie, still puzzled and shaken by his anger. For it was clearly directed at her. She strove for normality: 'Pull up a chair and I'll introduce you.' And as Zak moved to lift the chair towards the desk, Annie signed to Jill that Zak wanted to ask some questions.

After shaking hands with Jill, Zak casually turned to Annie and asked to see the questions that Annie had already asked. 'Fiona told me Jill is deaf and non-verbal; presumably you showed her enough courtesy to write down the questions?'

'Zak, why are you looking at me like this?' Annie whispered. 'What's wrong?'

'If you think hard enough, you'll realise. Now, Annie, the list of questions, please.'

'I . . I . . . ' Hurt and bewildered, Annie shook her head. She couldn't think straight with Zak's scornful, freezing eyes penetrating her.

'I see.' He reached for the pad and flicked a couple of pages — blank apart from the address and email Annie had asked Jill to write down, and the two finger positions Jill had drawn to point out Annie's mistake.

'You haven't even attempted to conduct an interview.' He spoke without moving his lips, keeping his face turned away from Jill.

Obviously sensing something was badly wrong, Jill reached across the table and touched Annie's hand to attract her attention. 'Do you want me to go?' she signed.

Making an immense effort, Annie smiled, shook her head and signed back: 'No. But I'll have to go. Can I come to your house tonight?' She wanted to carry on with the interview; she was almost sure Jill would be the ideal person for the catering.

Jill nodded and signed, 'Come at seven, I'll prepare a bullet.' Annie smiled again, more naturally this time; then, without looking at or speaking to Zak, stood up, unhooked her bag from where it was hanging on her chair, and managed a dignified exit.

Once she'd shut the door behind her, she leant on it and pressed her fingers against her eyes to push back the tears of despair. How could Zak think so badly of her? How could he have thought she'd not interviewed Jill? 'You haven't even attempted to conduct an interview.' That's what he'd said.

Annie stood there for a moment, taking deep gasping breaths, fighting for control, until she heard a noise from the other side of the door; the noise of a chair scraping on the floor. By now, Zak would have realised how he'd misjudged her. He was probably coming to find her.

Well, she didn't want to see him. Not now, not ever again. Desperation lent speed to her legs; in no time at all she was out of the building and starting up the Jeep.

10

The Jeep. Annie hadn't realised it could go so fast, didn't realise in fact that she was in danger of breaking the speed limit as she drove through Darlington; until, glancing in the mirror, she observed a police car coming up behind her. Then she slowed down to her usual sedate speed.

'Fancy thinking Zak might follow me.' She laughed hollowly. Oh, he had to make some pretence of coming to find her; he wouldn't have wanted Jill to see him in a bad light. After all, even if she couldn't hear what he'd said to Annie, it would have been pretty obvious what he thought.

She'd have realised he was looking on that pad for written questions. Well, if Jill's catering matched her personality, Annie would make sure she got the job before she left.

Yes. She was going to leave. If Gail and Martyn wouldn't have her back, if Zak made it hard for her to get another job, she'd manage somehow. She had some savings, and an aunt had left her some jewellery. She'd just have to sell a few pieces if necessary.

It's Friday tomorrow, mused Annie. Zak will be away all day because he's going with Edward, and one of the ground engineers we took on last week to look over the Dornier he's planning on buying. Seeing as I'll have the unexpected chance to sample Jill's cooking this evening, if she answers the rest of my questions the way I'm hoping she will, I can write her an official job offer tomorrow. Then . . .

Then, on Saturday, I'll pack my things and go. Zak wasn't expecting me to work this weekend, said I deserved it off because we've worked the last few. He won't know I've gone until Monday.

★　★　★

Two hours later Annie was ensconced in the kitchen at High Moor House. On the table lay the big heavy book she used for pressing flowers. Each selection of flowers lay in between two sheets of blotting paper. Also on the table was a colourful selection of thick, dripless candles.

She'd set a large oblong baking tin containing cubes of clear paraffin wax on the simmering plate of the Aga and, while she waited for the wax to melt, she opened the book to select some pressed flowers. She always found her hobby therapeutic, and today — after the hour of stormy weeping she'd indulged in on reaching the haven of the house — she more than needed something to do which would calm her.

Besides, flowering candles would make a nice gift to give to Jill tonight. Annie decided to use pansies on a yellow candle, and buttercups on a red one. When the wax had melted, holding a candle at either end, she touched part of it to the surface of the hot wax.

Then, using tweezers, she carefully lifted a pansy and placed it onto the candle where the hot wax had made contact.

She kept dipping and adding flowers; then finally, and with expertise, rolled the candle over the surface of the hot wax to coat the decoration.

Having finished the two for Jill, she made another two for Jackie. Then she stood for a long minute, biting hard on her lower lip. 'I must be some sort of masochist, but I've got to do it,' she muttered. 'And in time to come it will remind me of how stupid I was to fall in love with a heartless, arrogant, despicable brute.'

So, taking a deep breath, she forced herself to find the lilies-of-the-valley she'd pressed. What was it Colette had said that night in the restaurant? Maybe they'd be a happy memento . . . *Huh. If this was happy, she never wanted to do unhappy.*

It wasn't the best flowering candle she'd made. Her fingers had trembled too much, and her fast-flowing tears had blurred her vision, and all the cruel taunts Zak had made were echoing in her head . . . in her heart.

But mingling with the echoes was a memory of her first evening here when Zak had arrived to take her to Jackie and Bill's. She could picture again the moon shining above the lone tree in the garden, the front door open, and Zak telling her she looked like the Spirit of Autumn. Could remember all too clearly his warm mouth and the little ghost kisses whispering over her face.

He'd soon regretted that. And he'd accused her of wrecking people's lives. Well, she certainly seemed to have wrecked her own life. What would she do if Gail and Martyn wouldn't have her back?

Suddenly she remembered Violet telling her that if ever she needed a place to run to . . . She could go to Amsterdam for a while. Maybe get a job there. Yes, that was what she should do. She'd be bound to see Zak again if she went back to Edmunds'.

This decision didn't really help the despair she felt, but she pretended it did; pretended she'd enjoy the challenge, told herself she was glad she'd made up her mind to do something positive.

Finding pen, paper and an envelope, she sat down and wrote to Violet, giving her home address in Suffolk — for she'd be back there by the time Violet replied. She wrote the envelope and gazed at it for a moment before leaving it on the table. There. She'd post it on her way to Jill's tonight.

Next, what could be more positive than tidying and cleaning the house ready for her departure? There were still a couple of hours before she needed to get ready to go out. She'd start here in the kitchen. But first, she'd go into the garden and pick some fronds of the bracken which grew either side of the gates. It was a marvellous autumn shade of yellow-brown; she'd arrange it in the box she'd chosen to put Jill's candles in.

Annie was kneeling on the damp ground, bracken over her thighs, and once more she was unable to stem her flow of tears. For the last frond of bracken she'd picked had revealed a hibernating snail nestled snugly against the stone wall. 'Am I always going to be haunted by memories?' she murmured.

'Annie?' She heard her name spoken softly almost ghostily, and closed her eyes for a brief moment. It can't be, she told herself. I'm imagining it. She opened her eyes and knew the two leather-clad feet next to her thigh weren't in her imagination, and neither was the long length of body she allowed her gaze to travel up: dark trousers, leather jerkin . . .

'What are you doing here?' She leapt up, scattering the bracken as she did so, and glared stormily at Zak.

'You're crying,' he said softly and moved his hand towards her face.

'Don't touch me. Don't you dare touch me.' All her anger came to the fore; here was the man who'd hurt her beyond reason, the man who was driving her away with his unaccountable dislike, the man she hated. No, heaven help her, the man she loved. The man who must never get an inkling of her true feelings.

Frantically, she held on to her anger, then encouraged it, whipped it up into a frenzy.

'And I'm not crying,' she denied vehemently. 'There was something in my eye. I'm sorry to disappoint you, Zak, but it would take more than you misjudging me to make me cry. After all, I'm used to you thinking the worst of me, used to you jumping to wrong conclusions about me.

'I feel sorry for you, do you know that? Sorry for you, wrapped inside that bitter shell. For that's all you are, Zak, a shell of bitterness and ... No, Zak. Don't touch me.'

One arm snaked out and pulled her against him; the fingers of his other hand took hold of her chin. For a long breathless second he looked deep into her eyes and she tried to move her head, her body.

But it was a token gesture: she wanted his arm around her, wanted to feel him close, wanted his mouth on hers. Needed to taste his lips for one more time. For the last time.

He lowered his face to hers and whispered those remembered ghost kisses over her eyes . . . whispered, too, her name. 'Annie.'

What was she doing, allowing this . . . responding so willingly to this man who despised her? And what was he doing kissing her when all he felt for her was contempt? Oh, heavens, she had to find the strength to stop him. He was enslaving her — capturing her mind, her heart, her soul.

She recognised with her last ounce of sanity that if she wasn't careful he'd guess how she felt about him; guess that she loved him. His kiss deepened, causing dozens of fireworks to ignite inside her.

Denying the voice of reason, she

delighted in the devastating fire he'd lit within her as her fingers wandered over the back of his neck, revelling in the texture of his hair.

She whimpered in protest, her eyes flying open as his lips left hers, and he firmly removed her hands from around his neck. His breathing was ragged, and dark bands of colour seared his cheekbones. She could see his mouth moving as he spoke but his words didn't register.

'Could I trouble you to move the Jeep?' This other voice — a stranger's voice tinged with amusement — did register; and, dazedly, Annie turned her head to face the speaker.

'I've come to fill up your oil tank, Miss; it's round the side there and I can't get my wagon past the Jeep.'

'Fill up the oil tank?' Annie echoed, staring in bewilderment over the grey wall at the top of the wagon. How could a great big thing like that have driven up without her hearing?

Her face burnt as she silently

answered that question. She'd been oblivious to everything except Zak's lips and her own response to him.

'The Aga runs off oil,' Zak reminded her.

'And I need to get to the tank, only there's a Jeep in my way.'

Annie, to cover her embarrassment, glared at the delivery man and reminded him he'd already told her that once.

He, presumably not at all put out by her glare, said patiently, 'If you want the oil, you'll have to move the Jeep.'

With a muttered oath, Zak asked Annie where the keys for the Jeep were, and then strode off into the kitchen to get them. Annie pointedly turned her back on the delivery man and bent down to pick up the scattered fronds of bracken.

Soon she heard the Jeep start up, then the wagon; and, hoping Zak would supervise the filling of the oil tank, she made a beeline for the kitchen.

How could I have responded to Zak like that? she berated herself, throwing the bracken on to the table and moving to the sink to splash her burning cheeks with cold water.

How on earth was she going to face Zak when he came in?

How dare he do that to her? How dare he act like that when he always thought the worst of her? Well, he wouldn't be coming back in. She'd go outside and lock the back door behind her, then tell him to go and leave her alone. She couldn't handle this . . . this seesawing of emotions . . .

She'd left it too late. As she flung down the towel, Zak strolled into the kitchen and, pulling a chair out, sat down at the table. 'How come the Jeep wasn't parked down in the barn?'

It was the last thing Annie had expected him to say; all thoughts of not knowing how to face him disappeared and, hands on her hips, she placed herself by his chair and stared angrily at him.

'It's nothing to do with you where I park the Jeep.'

'Correction. It's everything to do with me. If it's left outside here it could get stolen. Isolated farms and houses, where any vehicle is likely to be a four-wheel-drive, are known to be a favourite target for car thieves.'

'If you're worried about vehicles parked outside, I suggest *you* get in yours and drive it away,' she retorted.

'I parked on the garage forecourt in the village. I didn't want — '

'You didn't want to be seen visiting me . . . is that what you were going to say? Afraid your precious Fiona might get to hear of it?'

'What's that supposed to mean?'

'You spend most of your spare time with her, Zak. She's always telling me where you've been together, or — '

'Together with Jackie and Bill. I do spend a fair amount of time with them, they're good friends. Fee is like another young sister to me. She always has been.'

'Perhaps you should tell her that's how you see her. She certainly thinks there's more to it.'

'I'm sure you're wrong. But I'll certainly make sure Fiona has no reason to think that.'

'I almost feel sorry for her,' Annie said.

'Sarcasm isn't your usual line, Annie. Anyone would think you were jealous of Fiona.'

Then he groaned. 'This is ridiculous. Look.' He ran his fingers through his hair and, scraping the chair back, stood up. Pacing around the kitchen, he resumed, 'I didn't intend what happened outside to happen, but unfortunately it did. When I came in after seeing to the delivery of oil I was going to apologise, but somehow I couldn't. It would have been insulting — '

'Huh.' Annie snorted. 'Since when has insulting me bothered you?'

Ignoring her interruption he carried on: 'I just said the first words that came into my head; and you, quite rightly, responded with anger. It isn't anything to do with me where you park the Jeep.'

He stopped pacing and stood in front of her looking down at her. 'The reason I left mine in the village was because I thought if you saw me driving up to the house, you'd refuse to let me in.

'I had to see you, Annie, had to apologise for the things I said, for the way I acted back in your office.' *And for how I've treated you at other times, too, and to ask your forgiveness,* he added silently.

'I should know by now that someone as gentle and caring as you . . . I knew even before I saw you using sign language to talk to Jill that I'd made a terrible mistake. It's no excuse, I know, but when I walked in and heard you say, 'Gosh. What an idiot', it — '

'Don't tell me,' Annie interrupted dully, wearily lowering herself on to the chair. 'It reminded you of Vicky, and — '

'Vicky? You've lost me, Annie.'

'Whenever anything reminds you of your sister, you take it out on me for some reason.'

210

'It didn't remind me of Vicky. I thought . . . although I quickly realised my mistake . . . I thought you were calling Jill an idiot.'

'That . . . that's even worse,' said Annie. 'I mean, it soon became obvious you thought I wasn't interviewing Jill, but for you to think I'd call her an idiot . . . '

'You were saying it just as I came into the office,' Zak said apologetically.

'I know. I remember. I thought you'd heard it, but knew I was calling *myself* an idiot. Thought maybe Vicky called herself names like that, and so you thought of her, and . . . '

Annie shrugged. 'Whatever. I can't take any more of it, Zak. You said you came to apologise; well, you've done that, and now you can leave. I mean it, Zak. I want you to leave right now.'

'Annie.' Zak pulled another chair out and sat down facing her. 'Annie, I know I've no right to ask, not after the way I've treated you, but please don't go. Oh, yes, I guessed you'd be thinking of

211

leaving even before I saw this when I came in to get the keys for the Jeep.'

He gestured towards the sealed envelope addressed to Violet.

'You've written to ask if you can go and stay with her?'

Annie nodded.

'Please don't go, Annie,' he said again. 'There are things I want to tell you. Things I must explain, though I need a bit more time to come to terms with it first.'

He ran his fingers through his hair. 'I imagine it'll be late evening before I get back from seeing the Dornier tomorrow, and I've promised to man Jackie's stall at the Farmers' Market on Saturday morning. But may I come here in the afternoon so we can talk? Please?'

Annie could feel herself weakening. It was the 'please' that had done it. She clamped her lips together to stop herself from replying.

Zak reached out and picked up the flowering candle she'd made with the lily-of-the-valley. 'I can't believe you won't let me,' he said. 'After all, you cared enough to save our flowers and turn them into something beautiful.'

Do I listen to my heart or my head? Annie asked herself, looking into his eyes. Haunted eyes, like a man in torment. Eyes I want to see full of love. Love for me. I want him to love me as I love him. Is there a chance, could there possibly be a chance of him feeling the same way? Dare I wait and see? Dare I *not* wait and see?

'Well?' Zak asked softly.

'I need time too, Zak. Time to think about my answer. Will you go now? I promise, if I stick to my decision to leave, I'll phone you Saturday morning to let you know. I can't say any more than that for now.'

He didn't move for a while, and the ensuing silence was broken only by the sound of him breathing and the dripping of the cold water tap into the sink. Out of desperation, Annie began to silently count the drips; she knew if she spoke it would be to tell him she'd stay. And she needed to think about it before she gave in to her heart.

Perversely, when Zak finally rose and left without a word, Annie wanted to call him back.

11

Annie had just got out of the Jeep when Anthony, the Chief Engineer, hurried towards her.

'I've got a bit of a problem,' he said ruefully. 'It's my wedding anniversary tomorrow. I've booked a table for the evening, but no way will I have time to go into town and buy a present today. I've so much work on you wouldn't believe.

'Can you think of anywhere local I might be able to get something suitable, apart from flowers and chocolates? It doesn't have to be big and expensive, just something to show I've remembered.'

'How about flowering candles?' Annie explained what she meant. 'Making them is a hobby of mine. I made some yesterday and I've two spare.' She was thinking of the two she'd made for Jackie, but if they'd solve Anthony's problem . . .

'They sound perfect, Annie. Could I call round for them this evening after I've finished here?'

Nodding, Annie gave him directions; and, smiling, Anthony hurried away back to the hangars.

As she walked into the *Edmunds' Airways North* building, Annie sighed. Everything here was coming together so well; she'd really like to see the job through to the end.

Jill had put on a marvellous spread last evening — shown she could turn simple-sounding salads into something out of this world, and the selection of tiny cakes had been delicious.

She'd even made a chocolate cake in the shape of a gun, and decorated it with bullets! Before leaving Jill's house, Annie had told her the job was hers, but warned her that she herself might not be staying.

Jill had smiled and, fingers flying, signed that Zak was worth staying for and true love never ran smooth.

But if he feels anything for me, then why does he need time to come to terms with it? Annie asked herself now, as she went into her office.

Jackie mentioned someone breaking up with Zak because she was jealous of his protectiveness towards Vicky. Was it because Vicky still needed him, and he thought that if he did have any feelings for Annie, she might resent Vicky, too?

But that didn't explain the 'coming to terms with it' thing. So —

A tap on the office door, followed by Fiona walking in, stemmed Annie's thoughts. The younger girl didn't look her usual self at all. But before Annie had time to ask if there was something wrong, Fiona spoke.

'The Job Centre phoned. They've three wanting to be interviewed for the receptionist's position. Shall I fix things for today?'

'I could see one this morning and two this afternoon,' said Annie. It was rushing things a bit, but *if* she was leaving, maybe she could appoint a receptionist first.

'Oh, and they asked if Jill came yesterday,' Fiona added. 'Apparently, she was there yesterday when the details were phoned through. That's how she arrived so quickly. I'm sorry I was so silly about her, Annie, I felt awful afterwards.'

'Don't worry about it, you'll be all right next time you see her. I'm offering her the catering contract. Could tell them at the Job Centre when you phone them back, please?'

Fiona nodded. 'I won't be seeing her again, though. I won't be coming back after today. Perhaps you should let the Job Centre know there's also a vacancy for a secretary.'

'I knew you were only temporary, but I thought you were hoping to become permanent?'

'That was when I thought there could be something between me and Zak,' Fiona replied, with a catch in her voice. 'He made it perfectly clear last night I was just like another sister to him. A *young* sister.'

Fiona dashed away a tear. 'I can't stay now I know he'll never love me. I just can't.'

'What will you do?' Annie asked. 'If you need a reference, I'll — '

'I'll go back to being the farm's secretary for Mum and Dad. Though I might think of moving to a place of my own. Zak calls in so often, it would *hurt* seeing him.'

'I'm sorry, Fiona,' Annie said. And she really was. She could emphathise so well with unrequited love. But, unlike Fiona, she didn't know for sure what Zak felt for her, did she? Maybe she should let him come round tomorrow and explain things.

A van pulling up outside broke the silence, and Annie glanced towards the window. 'The carpet fitters are here. You go and make yourself a coffee, Fiona, and I'll see to them.'

The rest of the day passed in a whirl of interviews, phone calls and discussions with the carpet fitters.

Once the fitters had gone, Annie decided to give the carpets a light vacuuming. She knew some people said you should give them time to settle first, but there was quite a lot of fluff about.

'I've just come to say it'll be around seven o'clock before I get to yours, Annie,' Anthony said loudly — speaking over the noise of the vacuum cleaner when he walked into the office.

Annie switched the cleaner off. 'I'll have coffee and candles ready,' she said. She knew Anthony liked the same strong coffee as she did.

'You're a sweetheart.' Anthony blew her a kiss; then, turning to go, almost collided with Fiona.

'I'm off now, Annie,' the younger girl said. 'I hope you have a nice evening,' she added, before hurrying away.

Tidying through the house in case I decide to leave it in the morning, Annie thought, after calling goodbye to Fiona. Sighing, she pushed the vacuum cleaner into a corner, then picked up her bag.

Before she went home, she walked round slowly, saying a silent goodbye to everything in case she didn't return.

Driving the Jeep still took all her concentration, so she couldn't allow herself to think of Zak.

But by the time she'd walked to High Moor House, after parking 'Monster' in the barn, Zak was all she could think about. Maybe, even if he did get back late, he'd phone her? Hearing his voice might help her decision.

After Anthony had collected the candles, she made something to eat, and then tidied around. And, although she vacuumed in short bursts — so she wouldn't miss the phone ringing — and although she stayed up until well past midnight, there was no call from Zak.

★ ★ ★

'Go or stay? Go or stay?' Annie muttered as she got out of bed. She just couldn't make up her mind.

Glancing out of the window she

221

noticed a weak November sun shining like a feeble lantern over the not-so-distant moors, and decided to go for a walk. If she was leaving, she might as well get a one time use out of her walking boots before she went.

Half an hour later, she was on her way down the winding track, making for another track off that one that led upwards to the moors.

Before she reached it, she saw Zak, driving towards her in the Bristol. He must have told Jackie he couldn't man the market stall. And that must mean, because I didn't phone him to say I'm leaving, he couldn't wait until this afternoon to see me, thought Annie.

And, heart singing, she stepped close in to the verge and he drew up alongside her. But, wait a minute. He didn't look exactly pleased to see her.

'I got home earlier than I expected last night, Annie,' he said through the open window. 'I really needed to see you, so I thought I'd take a chance and call on you.'

'You should have done,' Annie said, stooping close to the window.

'Oh, I did. It was just gone seven when I got to High Moor House and saw a car I recognised parked outside. I realised you must be busy, so I drove away again.'

He's at it again, Annie thought furiously. Hinting, implying there was something going on — this time between me and Anthony. Well, I've had enough. I won't stand here and listen to his accusations . . .

Straightening, she edged her way past the car, and then started to run.

She heard him call her name over the sound of her pounding feet, and then heard the soft purr of the Bristol's engine.

Her job had trained her to think clearly in a panic situation, and her training came to the fore now. She'd got to get off this track and onto the one up to the moors. He wouldn't chance driving up there.

And here was that track. Up and up

she ran, stumbling over rough tussocks and uneven ridges. Then, as often happened in this area, the weather changed in a flash and it started to rain. Cold, deluging November rain,

Her hair flew out around her head and whipped cruelly into her eyes, but she kept running. Clarity of mind had deserted her now; she was sobbing, her tears, the driving rain and cold, wet strands of hair blinding her.

She tripped, fell to her knees, got up, carried on, and heard Zak's voice calling her name. He must have left the car on the track below and followed her. She glanced over her shoulder; and this time, when she fell, she hadn't got the strength to get up.

Face-down she lay there, breathing in the scent of the earthy, wintry-wet moor. The tussock dug into her face, and in a weird sort of way she welcomed the pain.

Then there was a different sort of pain as, through her padded anorak, she felt hard fingers gripping her shoulders, trying to turn her over. She resisted but her resistance wasn't strong enough; she could feel his warm breath on her face, smell his elusive male scent . . .

All right, he'd managed to turn her over, but he couldn't make her open her eyes; couldn't make her look at him.

Then his fingers, gentle now, moved the strands of hair from her face, and traced a delicate path over her closed eyes and down her cheeks. 'Annie, Annie, are you hurt? Speak to me, please speak to me.'

He'd sounded worried, really worried. She opened her eyes and looked at him. Was that love and caring she could see in his eyes?

'You took what I said the wrong way, Annie. I was upset I'd seen Anthony's car parked outside High Moor House because I thought you'd invited him round for a farewell drink. Thought you'd decided you'd leave without giving me a chance to talk to you.'

The expression on his face left no doubt in her mind that he was telling the truth. She *had* taken his words the wrong way, *had* overreacted. But if she stayed, would it always be like this — with one of them misunderstanding something the other did or said?

'I still haven't made up my mind, Zak. I . . . I think I would like to hear what you've got to say before I do.'

'Well, I don't think this is the best place for me to try and explain everything,' he said. 'We could both end up with pneumonia if we stay here much longer. Besides, I've left the car blocking the track. Come on, Annie. Let's get you back to High Moor House and we'll talk.'

He kept her hand firmly in his as they trundled silently down to where he'd left the car.

★   ★   ★

'We can't sit around in these wet clothes,' said Annie as they walked into the kitchen — the warmth a welcome relief. She wriggled out of her anorak, placed it over the rail on the Aga and watched Zak shrugging off his jacket and putting it next to hers.

'I've got a large towelling bathrobe,' she told him. 'You'd better change into that. It will be a bit short but at least you'll be more comfortable.' She knew her voice had sounded husky, and just hoped Zak would put it down to the fact she was cold and wet.

And of course, that's what the huskiness was down to. It was nothing to do with the thought of what Zak would be wearing — or not wearing . . .

'Thanks, I'll do that. Change into your bathrobe,' he said, and Annie realised she must have looked startled or vague. 'Funny how often we find ourselves talking when water of some kind or other has soaked one or both of us,' he added, with the half smile that tugged at her heartstrings.

'I'll fetch it down. You can sort yourself out in here while I'm getting into dry clothes upstairs.'

Annie took her time over changing.

As much as she wanted to hear what Zak had to tell her, she needed time to get her emotions under control.

Eventually, though, after a few deep breaths, she made her way downstairs and back into the kitchen.

'I've made us a coffee. I hope that's OK?' Zak said, looking immensely appealing with his hair roughed up and her bathrobe just about covering his knees.

'Great, thanks,' she replied.

'Well, let's sit at the table, and I'll get on with what I need to say,' he said tersely.

She wondered if she should reply jokingly to lighten the atmosphere. Something like: 'Your wish is my command.' But, deciding against that, she just said, 'Right,' and then walked to the table, pulled out a chair and sat on it.

'I didn't know it at the time, but I suppose it really started when I approached Gail and Martyn about a partnership,' Zak began once he, too, had settled at the table with his cup of coffee.

228

'I'd sold my business and I was looking for a new venture. It was actually Vicky's husband who suggested Edmunds' Airways. He always flew 'The Edmunds' Way'.

'I didn't know they desperately needed a cash injection, but once they realised I was serious, they didn't hold anything back.'

Annie nodded. Gail and Martyn hadn't let their employees know they were in financial difficulties, but they weren't the sort to try and hide anything from a prospective business partner.

'I came down here every ten days or so. The first discussions all took place at a hotel or at their house,' Zak continued. 'After a few such meetings, Gail suggested that if things went ahead and we opened a northern branch, you'd be the ideal person to approach to help set things up.'

Annie nodded again; she'd made up her mind not to comment or interrupt him if she could help it.

'Gail showed me your file and I

agreed that somebody like you would make our task a lot easier. I think you were on holiday at the time. Afterwards, Gail never thought to mention you were off with a broken ankle. She probably knew you'd be back before the final decision was made.

'As things came close to being settled, I obviously needed to spend time at Edmunds' on normal working days. That didn't happen as soon as we'd planned because Vicky had her accident and needed me around.'

Zak drained his coffee mug and poured himself another from the cafetière.

'Although she and my brother-in-law live in Suffolk, only half-an-hour's drive away from Edmunds', for the first few days I wouldn't have felt happy leaving her while I spent time there.'

Unable to help herself, Annie reached across the table and touched his hand in sympathy. 'It must have been a worry-ing time.'

'It was. Anyway, there came the day when I felt I could leave her. That was the day we first met — when you were moving that snail.' He gave a brief smile. 'Only of course, I didn't find out who you were until later.'

'You thought I was an irresponsible teenager,' said Annie, forgetting again she'd vowed not to comment on anything.

Zak clearly decided to ignore her words.

'I'd already told Gail I wanted to meet the employee whose file I'd read without her knowing who I was or why I was there. I wanted to judge for myself whether she'd be able to cope with the responsibility of helping set up a new branch. And I needed to see if we were compatible. I knew we'd be working very closely together.'

'So Edmunds' birthday celebration was used as a cover,' said Annie. 'Gail let me think you were from the Ministry,' she added. 'I played right into your hands there.'

'But we didn't have time for much talking at the party, did we? Poor Violet saw to that. Though seeing the way you handled the whole situation, how gentle you were with Violet, how you managed to keep her calm, I was sure I wanted you working by my side.'

'But you took me for that meal to make double-sure?'

'I still had questions I needed answering, Annie. Gail had already told me how you'd come to be part of Edmunds', but I wanted to hear it from you too. And over that meal, we seemed to forge a bond between us.'

'Then something happened to break it.'

Zak's fingers toyed restlessly with his coffee mug. 'This is the bit I'm ashamed of, Annie. Where I need your understanding and forgiveness.'

Zak went on to tell her why Vicky had been upset, why she'd been driving to see him when she'd had her crash.

'I'm not sure I understand, Zak. I mean, you knew I'd unknowingly gone out with a married man, but . . . Do you mean you felt you had to blame every woman that had happened to for your brother-in-law having a relation-ship with another — '

'His name is Oliver. Vicky told me she thought Oliver used to meet his other woman when he went on business trips to Amsterdam. Then I heard Hildy telling you to forget Oliver, and . . . '

'It was after that obnoxious man had been chatting me up in front of his wife,' Annie recalled. 'Hildy thought I'd overreacted because I couldn't forget what I'd gone through when I found out Russell Oliver was married. Hildy always referred to him as 'Slimebag Oliver' after . . . '

Annie stared at Zak. 'I can under-stand how you thought what you did. What I can't understand is why you still wanted me to come up here and work with you?'

Zak laughed: a bitter, heart-rending sound. 'I was more determined than ever you should. I even hinted to Martyn the deal wouldn't go through if you weren't part of it. At that time you were still thinking I worked for the

Ministry, and wouldn't connect me with the new partner Gail and Martyn would tell you about.

'I knew I'd probably already let you see the bitter and angry side of me, so I warned Gail and Martyn not to mention my name in case you refused to work with someone with such mood swings.'

'I think I would have refused,' Annie admitted.

'As it was, Martyn told me you actually volunteered eagerly to help set up the northern branch. The devil in me gloried at that snippet. You'd made it easy for me.'

'Made what easy? I still don't understand.'

'Made it easy for me to take revenge for how you'd upset Vicky, caused her accident, probably wrecked her marriage. Of course, if I'd known at that point you'd been off for three months with your foot and leg in plaster, I'd never have thought it was you. When I worked things out after Gail mentioned your ankle, those three months coincided with the time Vicky had her first suspicions.'

Annie could tell from Zak's expression that he wanted her to say something. But a suffocating sensation had tightened her throat.

'I'm not explaining things very well,' said Zak. 'There's so much I need to tell you, Annie, I'm trying to say it all at once because when I've said it, I'll find out if you can forgive me.'

Annie swallowed hard, trying to clear her throat.

Zak obviously took the small sound as an indication to carry on.

'When you first came up here, I was still thinking it was you who'd caused Vicky's distress, and that's what this house in the middle of nowhere was all about. I wanted you to be frightened and lonely, the way I thought you'd made Vicky feel, though of course her feelings were for a different reason.

'The Jeep, the long working hours, crack-of-dawn starts . . . I wanted to make your life hell. But all along my heart kept telling me I was wrong. Wrong to be treating you the way I was, and wrong to think you'd lied.'

'Is that what you needed time to come terms with?'

'That and the fact I'd fallen in love with you, Annie.'

She could feel his eyes on her, but wouldn't — couldn't — look up.

'Despite of having what I thought was proof you were the one Oliver had been seeing,' he continued, 'I knew deep-down that couldn't be so. I felt sure you'd told the truth when you'd said you'd no idea the man you'd been seeing was married. Oliver's woman knew he was married.'

Annie reached for the cafetière. It was empty. Glad of a reason to move, she jumped up to boil the kettle again. She could understand why Zak had acted how he had; she could forgive him, too. She should be glorying in the fact her love was returned.

But it was looking more and more as

if the one Zak's brother-in-law had been seeing was Katie. Katie had covered for her during those three months — that was when she'd met the man who'd provided her with a flat. The man Katie had admitted wasn't free.

Katie had implied it was all over, though. Everything in her life had changed and she was busy with pantomime rehearsals in Bournemouth.

But, even if it was over, Annie was pretty sure Zak wouldn't allow himself to love her once he knew it was her sister who'd caused all Vicky's heartache.

Would there be any reason for Zak to know, though? Annie sighed as she reached for the boiling kettle. Could she keep something like that from him?

'Annie. For heaven's sake say something. Even if it's to tell me you're still going to leave.'

'How is Vicky now?' she asked, walking back to the table to get their used mugs and walking to the sink to rinse them.

'I think she's going to be all right. I hope so. She's giving Oliver another chance. He showed her a letter from the woman he'd been seeing. I'd already got past the stage of thinking it was you.

'Anyway, according to Vicky, this Lindy made it perfectly clear it really was all over. She even told Oliver she hoped he could mend his marriage.'

He groaned. 'I'll understand if you find it impossible to believe I *was* sure you weren't the one Oliver had been seeing, way before I knew her name was Lindy. But I swear to you, Annie, it's true.'

Filled with a dizzying sense of relief, Annie stumbled back to the table, half-fell onto her chair and buried her face in her hands. It wasn't her sister Oliver had been seeing. There was nothing to get in the way of Zak's feelings. That meant she could tell him . . .

She sensed a movement from Zak, and when she heard his chair scrape, she looked up.

'Your silence speaks for itself, Annie. I'm going now.'

'No.' Annie jumped up and went to stand in front of him. 'I forgive you, Zak, I love you. I love you more than anything else in this world. And . . . '

She waved a hand towards the candle she'd made. 'Maybe the lilies-of-the-valley were telling the truth.'

'Telling the truth?'

'They mean 'return of happiness'. If you meant it when you said you loved me then . . . '

'I meant it, Annie. But I can't believe you can love me after the things I once thought, after the way I've behaved.'

Standing on tiptoe, she put her arms around his neck and touched her lips to his — felt them warm and sweet on hers.

She quivered at the sweet tenderness; it was a kiss for her soul to melt into.

The magical, glorious, healing moment was broken by an urgent hammering on the front door.

They pulled apart and Annie groaned.

'Let's ignore it, and whoever it is will go away,' she said.

But the hammering became louder and more insistent. Impossible to ignore.

'I'll go,' Zak said. 'And I'll get rid of whoever it is quickly.'

Still feeling as though she was floating on a cloud, Annie watched him stride out of the kitchen. Fingers to mouth, she dreamily relived that sweet and tender kiss.

Astonishment brought her down to earth when she heard her sister's voice.

'So you're the reason Annie came to work up here. Gail gave me the address, but this little love nest wasn't easy to find.'

Annie flew into the hall. 'Katie. What on earth are you doing here?'

'Sorry if I've disturbed anything.' Katie glanced meaningfully at Zak.

'We got caught in the rain and had to change,' Annie said. 'But what are you doing here?' she repeated.

'I've come to see you, sweetie. What

else? But I'll tell you why when you've given me a coffee. Black, no milk or sugar. I've had a long drive. Is that the kitchen?' she added, walking towards the open door.

Glancing helplessly at each other, Annie and Zak followed her in and watched as Katie sat down at the table.

'I'll make the coffee,' Zak said.

Annie nodded her thanks before speaking again to her surprise visitor. 'Are you on a break from pantomime rehearsals?' she asked.

'I'm not doing the panto now, that's part of what I've come to tell you. It's probably upset a few people, me opting out. My understudy will take my part, though. But before I tell you the exciting parts . . . ' Katie waved a hand towards Zak. 'Aren't you going to introduce us, Annie? I'm guessing he's Edmunds' new partner Gail mentioned, though I never saw him while I was there covering for you when you broke your ankle. Even though I had my own love to keep me warm, I would have noticed him.'

'Zak, this is my sister, Katie,' Annie said, still somewhat in a daze.

'And here's your coffee, Katie.' Zak passed her the mug.

'Not Katie. I've gone back to using my full name all the time now. It's a much better name for an actress.'

Annie sighed. Katie clearly wanted to be the centre of attention for a while. 'Right. Zak, this is my sister, Kathleen.'

'No, not Kathleen; I changed it to another version by deed poll years ago.' She smiled up at Zak.

Walking round the table, Annie was about to pull out another chair so all three of them could sit down, when her sister spoke again.

'I'm Kate*lyn*, Zak, and I'm pleased to meet you.'

Annie had heard the expression 'blood freezing in the veins', and now she experienced it for herself as her fingers stayed clutched over the back of the chair.

Kate*lyn* . . . *Lindy*. Her original

thought of it having been her sister who'd caused Vicky's distress — and accident — had been right.

And Zak would surely realise that, too. Annie heard his sharp intake of breath and knew he did.

12

'Well, my stage name wasn't meant to cause a pause for effect, but it seems it has,' said Katie.

Annie was hurting too much to speak.

Even the fact Zak had moved to stand behind her — had put his arms around her waist — didn't alleviate her despair.

'Here's the part I thought would stun you, Annie. I'm off to America in a month. Have you heard of Oswald Oswold? He's a big name over there, and he's going to make me a movie star. Trenton, too. He's a friend of Trenton's.'

Annie was shocked out of her silence. 'Trenton? You mean — '

'Yes, my husband. We never did get divorced, you know. We just separated. We met unexpectedly when he flew to Amsterdam. It was my first day at Edmunds'. We started seeing each other, and then he suggested I should go and stay in the flat he was looking after while the owner was away.'

'You mean when you told me the man in your life was separated from his wife, it was *you* he was separated from? Your ex-husband was the new man in your life? Why didn't you tell me that?'

Katie shrugged. 'It felt like too big a deal to tell anyone. And Trenton isn't my ex-husband. I told you, Annie, we never got divorced. But he was seeing someone; so, at first, it felt as though *I* was his 'other woman' and not her. At the time, I thought it would be sort of good to have all the pluses and none of the minuses.'

After a struggle, Annie managed to uncurl her fingers, pull out the chair and sit down. Aware it was the second time she'd half-fallen onto a chair, she had to stop herself from giggling.

Relief must be making me hysterical, she thought, as she watched Zak pick up the chair he'd been sitting on earlier and walk round the table with it to sit down next to her.

'I soon realised I wanted the minuses

along with the pluses though,' her sister continued. 'You know: having to consider someone else before doing something, having to hurry up in the bathroom, pick smelly socks up off the floor . . . '

'So you and Trenton are properly together again, and you're both going to America hoping to become movie stars? Have I got it right?' Annie asked, staring at her sister.

'There's something happening before that, Annie. We're going to renew our vows. And this time, I'd like you to be there. Zak, too, if you like. It seems as if the two of you are special to each other.'

She smiled and pointed across the table to their clasped hands resting on it.

'Please, Annie,' she added. 'Please say you'll come to the ceremony.'

If she'd had the chance, Annie knew she'd say yes — just so her sister would go and she and Zak could be alone again.

Zak had put his arms around her *before* they'd heard the rest of Katie's tale — when he, too, must have been thinking Katie, who now called herself

246

Katelyn, was the Lindy his brother-in-law had been seeing.

That must mean he wouldn't have let that stop them from being together; wouldn't have made sure not to allow himself to love her. Annie wanted to tell him again how much she loved him. But Katie was still talking:

'I know I've never been much of a sister to you. I wasn't much of a daughter to Mum and Dad, either. I'm sorry. I've always been too self-centred and secretive, haven't I? Trenton told me that and he was right.'

Annie nodded. 'Why were you?'

'I think I was scared to share anything in case whatever it was turned out to be a failure. But I've grown up a bit now, and am trying to think of others as well as myself. And I thought maybe you might like to be there when Trenton and I renew our vows. If you need time to think, you've got three-and-a-half weeks.

'We got the date confirmed yesterday and I had to come and see you straight away. I couldn't have done this on the

247

phone or in a letter. I needed to be with you face to face, Annie. Needed to say sorry for the times I wasn't there for you, for the times I said hurtful things.'

'I'll come to the ceremony,' said Annie. 'But I'd like you to go now. Zak and I — '

'Go? Go where? I haven't booked anywhere, Annie. I thought you'd be able to give me a bed for the night.'

'Of course she will,' Zak said. 'But before she shows you to where you'll be sleeping . . . You did say your ceremony isn't for another three-and-a-half weeks?'

Katie nodded.

'If your sister, who I love more than words can say, agrees to marry me, what would you say to a double ceremony?'

Zak turned Annie's face to his. 'I hadn't planned on proposing in front of an audience. But, Annie, my one true love, will you marry me? And if you will, would you like to arrange it so Katie aka Katelyn can see you married before she goes off to America?'

'I'll find my own way upstairs to a

bedroom,' said Katie, jumping up. 'You two need to be alone. But . . . ' She bent over and whispered in Annie's ear. 'You'll break his heart and yours if you don't accept his proposal.'

In a daze again, Annie watched her sister hurry from the room. And again, Zak turned Annie's face to his.

'Speechless?' he asked, running a gentle finger down her cheek.

Annie gazed into his eyes for a long moment.

'I want lilies-of-the-valley for my wedding bouquet,' she whispered.

Zak didn't give her chance to say any more. Not that Annie minded.

Once more, she was lost in the velvet warmth of his kisses. And she knew the warmth of their love would last them their lifetime.

THE END